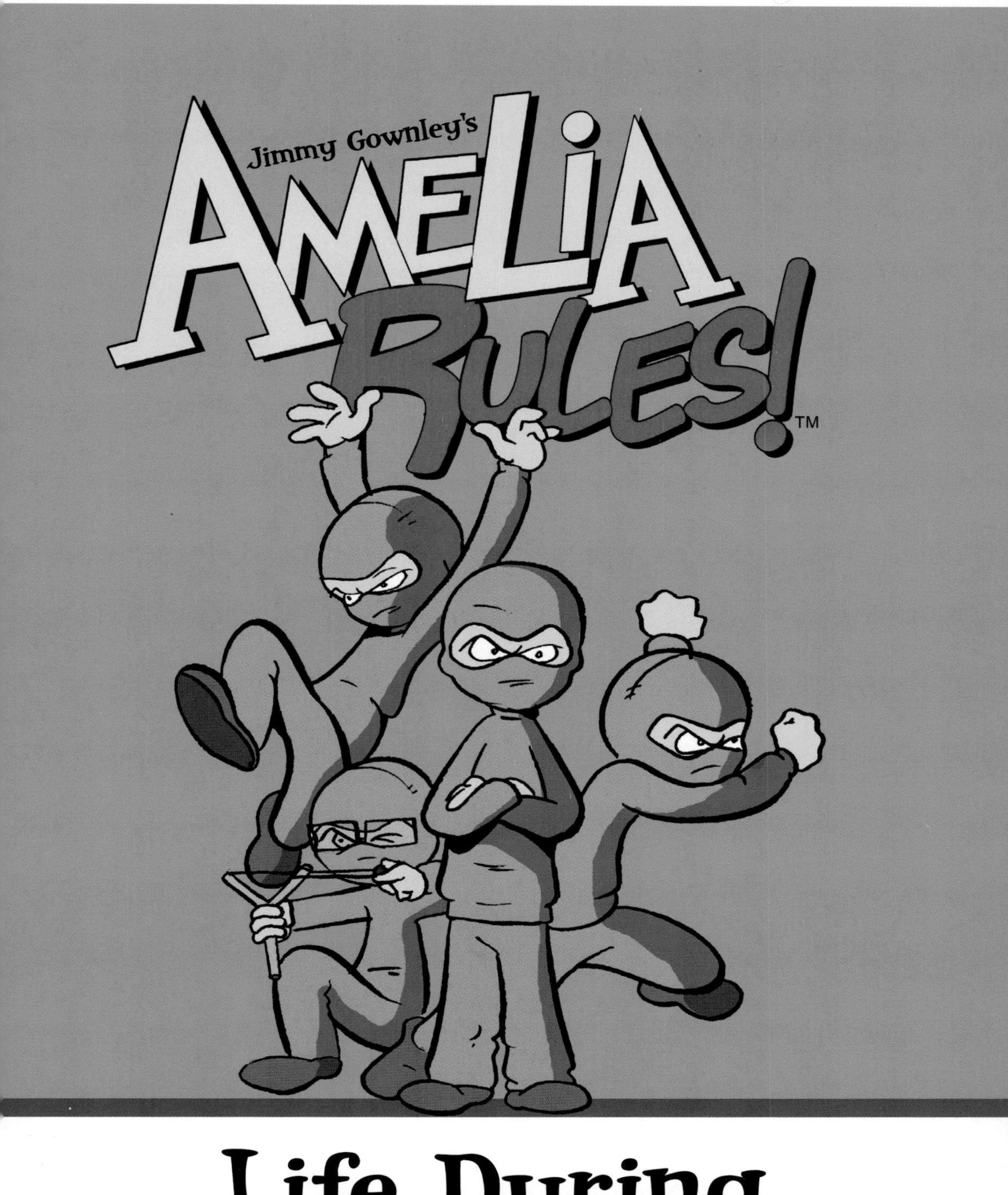
Jimmy Gownley's
AMELIA RULES!
TM

Life During Wartime

Atheneum Books for Young Readers
New York London Toronto Sydney
Spotlight

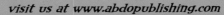

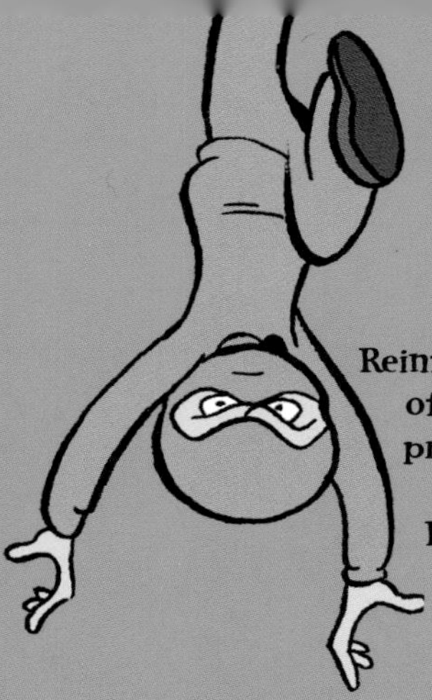

visit us at www.abdopublishing.com

Reinforced library bound edition published in 2013 by Spotlight, a division of the ABDO Group, PO Box 398166, Minneapolis, MN 55439. Spotlight produces high-quality reinforced library bound editions for schools and libraries. Published by agreement with Atheneum Books for Young Readers, an imprint of Simon & Schuster Children's Publishing Division.

Printed in the United States of America, North Mankato, Minnesota.

102012

012013

This book contains at least 10% recycled materials.

· Special thanks to Michael Cohen ·

This book is a work of fiction. Any references to historical events, real people, or real locales are used fictitiously. Other names, characters, places, and incidents are products of the author's imagination, and any resemblance to actual events or locales or persons, living or dead, is entirely coincidental.

Book design by Jimmy Gownley and Sonia Chaghatzbanian

Library of Congress Cataloging-in-Publication Data

Gownley, Jimmy.
Amelia's life during wartime / [Jimmy Gownley]. -- Reinforced library bound ed.
p. cm. -- (Jimmy Gownley's Amelia rules!)
Summary: Determined to conquer the ninjas and drive them out of a park, Reggie begins a campaign to recruit more members to the superhero club, G.A.S.P., which Amelia suspects is a bad idea.
ISBN 978-1-61479-073-0
1. Graphic novels. [1. Graphic novels. 2. Clubs--Fiction. 3. Interpersonal relations--Fiction.] I. Title.
PZ7.G69Aql 2013
741.5'973--dc23

2012026912

Spotlight

All Spotlight books are reinforced library bindings and manufactured in the United States of America.

To my beautiful girls:
Stella Mary and
Anna Elizabeth,
And to their wonderful mother, Karen.

You're what make ME happy.

MEET THE GANG

Amelia Louise McBride:
Our heroine. Wise cracking, yet sweet. She spends her time hanging out with friends and her aunt Tanner.

Reggie Grabinsky:
A.k.a. Captain Amazing. Founder of G.A.S.P., which he forces . . . er, encourages, his friends to join.

Rhonda Bleenie:
Smart, stubborn, and loud. She wears her heart on her sleeve and it's filled with love for Reggie.

Pajamaman:
Never speaks. Always cool. His feetie jammies tell you what's on his mind.

Tanner:
Amelia's aunt and a former rock 'n' roll superstar.

Amelia's Mom (Mary):
Starting a new life in Pennsylvania with Amelia after the divorce.

Amelia's Dad:
Still lives in New York, and
misses Amelia terribly.

G.A.S.P.
Gathering Of Awesome Super Pals.
The superhero club Reggie founded.

Park View Terrace Ninjas:
Club across town and nemesis
to G.A.S.P.

Kyle:
The main ninja. Kind of a jerk
but not without charm.

Joan:
Former Park View Terrace Ninja
(nemesis of G.A.S.P.), now friends
with Amelia and company.

Tweenie Zeenie:
A local kid-run magazine and Web site.

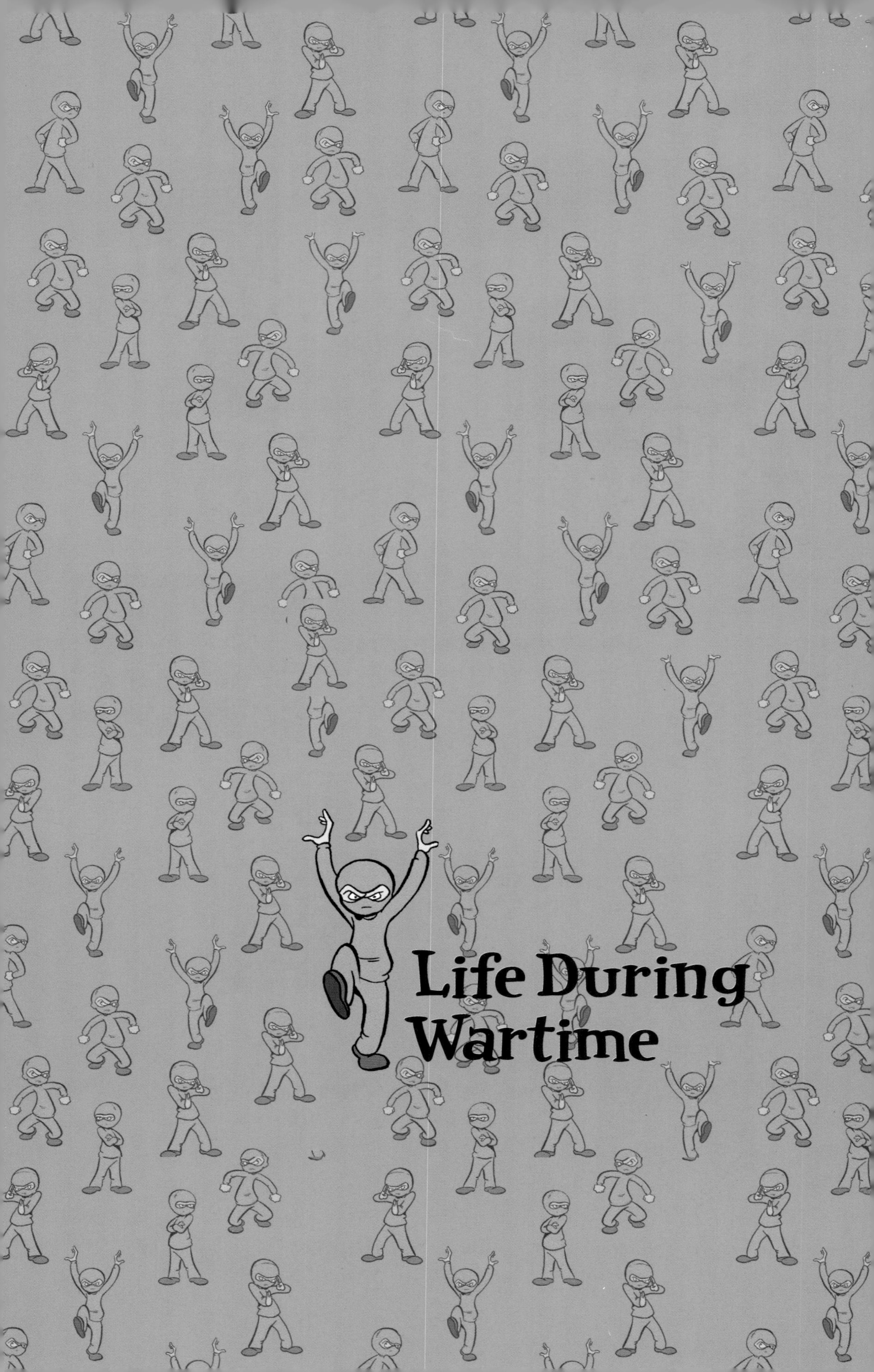
Life During
Wartime

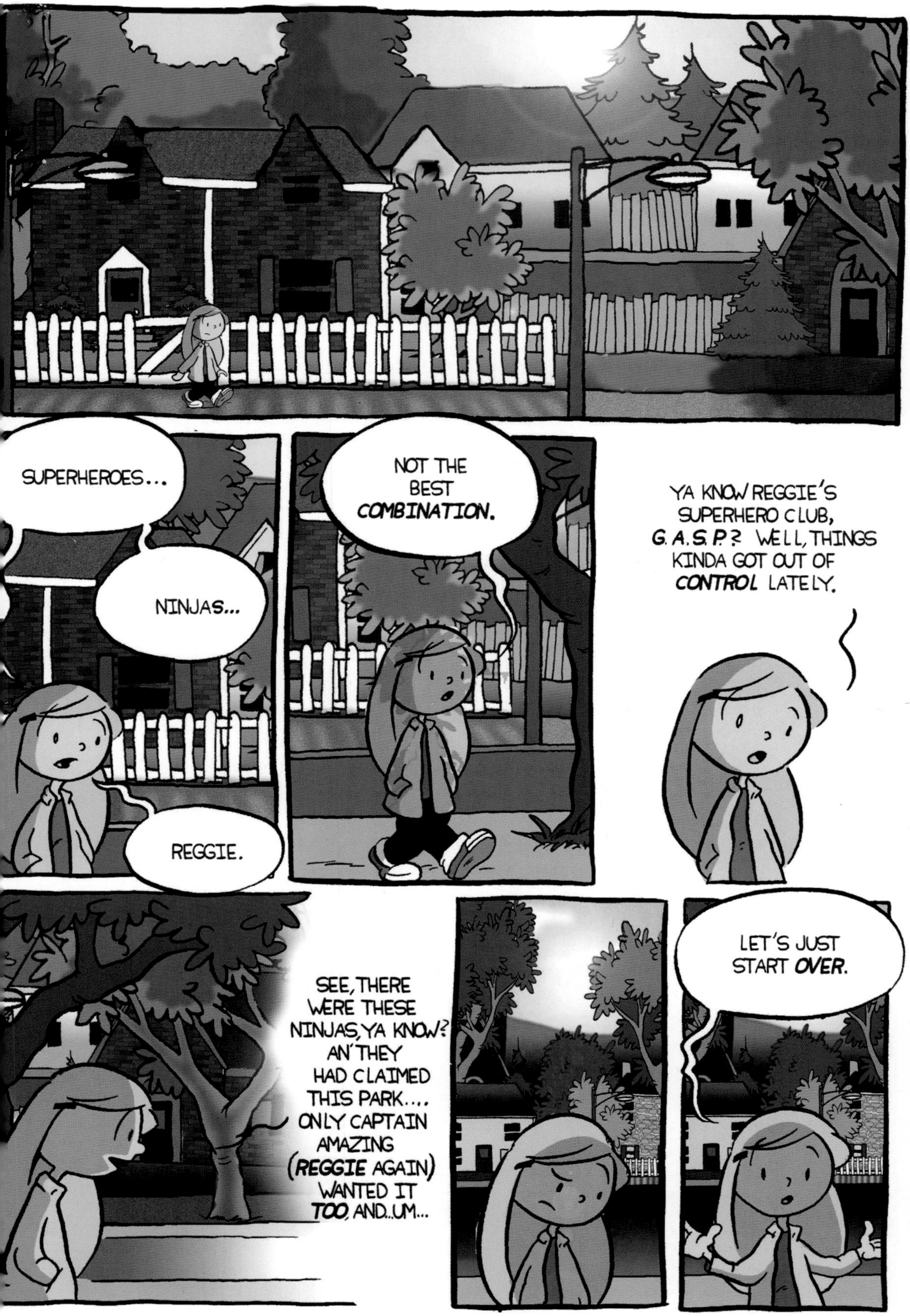
SUPERHEROES...
NINJAS...
REGGIE.
NOT THE BEST COMBINATION.
YA KNOW REGGIE'S SUPERHERO CLUB, G.A.S.P.? WELL, THINGS KINDA GOT OUT OF CONTROL LATELY.
SEE, THERE WERE THESE NINJAS, YA KNOW? AN' THEY HAD CLAIMED THIS PARK.... ONLY CAPTAIN AMAZING (REGGIE AGAIN) WANTED IT TOO, AND...UM...
LET'S JUST START OVER.

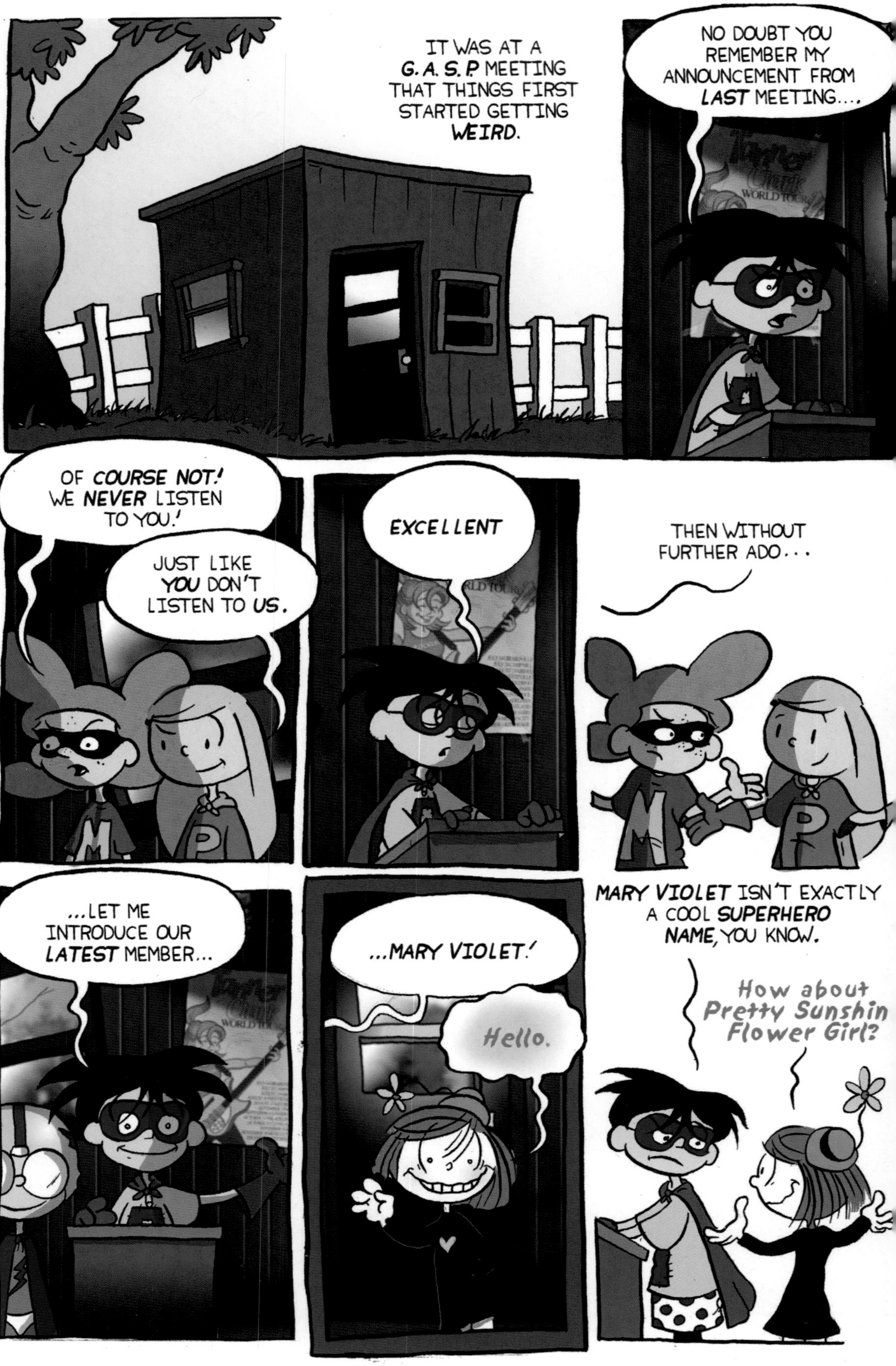
IT WAS AT A G.A.S.P. MEETING THAT THINGS FIRST STARTED GETTING WEIRD.
NO DOUBT YOU REMEMBER MY ANNOUNCEMENT FROM LAST MEETING....
OF COURSE NOT! WE NEVER LISTEN TO YOU!
JUST LIKE YOU DON'T LISTEN TO US.
EXCELLENT
THEN WITHOUT FURTHER ADO...
...LET ME INTRODUCE OUR LATEST MEMBER...
...MARY VIOLET!
Hello.
MARY VIOLET ISN'T EXACTLY A COOL SUPERHERO NAME, YOU KNOW.
How about Pretty Sunshin
Flower Girl?

THAT WASN'T *EXACTLY* WHAT REGGIE HAD IN MIND, *EITHER.*

I WAS PRETTY SURPRISED TO SEE *MARY VIOLET.*

SHE DIDN'T SEEM LIKE THE *MASKED AVENGER* TYPE.

HA! LITTLE DID I KNOW...

SO, *ANYWAY,* REGGIE WANTED *MARY* VIOLET TO BE IN THE CLUB.

BUT FIRST, SHE HAD TO PASS *THE TRIALS.*

SO REGGIE DRAGGED US ALL THE WAY *ACROSS TOWN*...

...TO THIS *PARK* HE AND *PAJAMAMAN* HAD FOUND.

I THINK HE LIKED IT CUZ HE COULD RUN AROUND WITH HIS UNDIES OUTSIDE HIS PANTS AND NO ONE WOULD KNOW HIM.

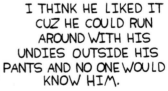

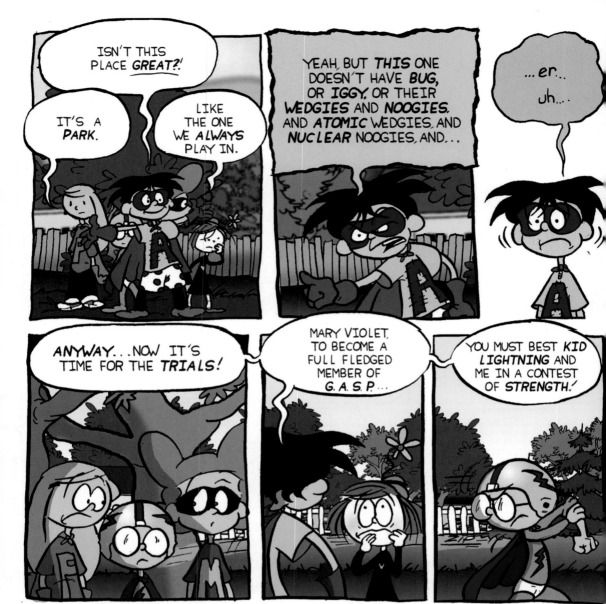

ISN'T THIS PLACE *GREAT?!*

IT'S A *PARK.*

LIKE THE ONE WE *ALWAYS* PLAY IN.

YEAH, BUT *THIS* ONE DOESN'T HAVE *BUG,* OR *IGGY,* OR THEIR *WEDGIES* AND *NOOGIES,* AND *ATOMIC* WEDGIES, AND *NUCLEAR* NOOGIES, AND...

...er... uh....

ANYWAY...NOW IT'S TIME FOR THE *TRIALS!*

MARY VIOLET, TO BECOME A FULL FLEDGED MEMBER OF *G.A.S.P.*...

YOU MUST BEST *KID LIGHTNING* AND ME IN A CONTEST OF *STRENGTH!*

PRINCESS POWERFUL, MISS MIRACULOUS, YOU BE THE *LOOKOUTS.*

DO YOU THINK SHE'LL BE *OKAY?*

I DON'T THINK SHE EVER *WAS* OKAY.

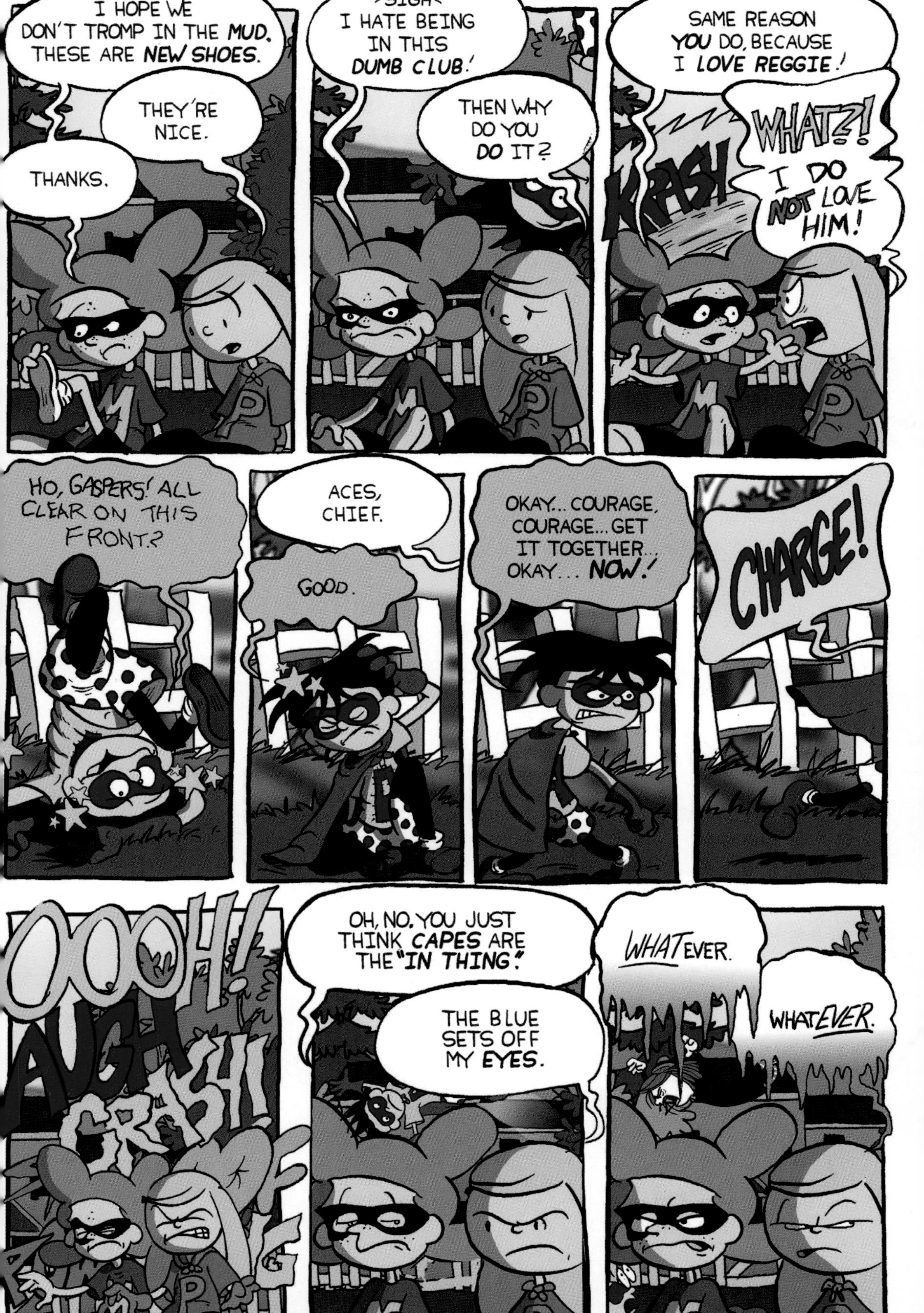

I HOPE WE DON'T TROMP IN THE MUD. THESE ARE NEW SHOES.
THEY'RE NICE.
THANKS.
>SIGH< I HATE BEING IN THIS DUMB CLUB!
THEN WHY DO YOU DO IT?
SAME REASON YOU DO, BECAUSE I LOVE REGGIE!
KRASH
WHAT?! I DO NOT LOVE HIM!
HO, GASPERS! ALL CLEAR ON THIS FRONT?
ACES, CHIEF.
GOOD.
OKAY... COURAGE, COURAGE... GET IT TOGETHER... OKAY... NOW!
CHARGE!
OOOH!
AUGH
CRASH!
OH, NO. YOU JUST THINK CAPES ARE THE "IN THING."
THE BLUE SETS OFF MY EYES.
WHATEVER.
WHATEVER.

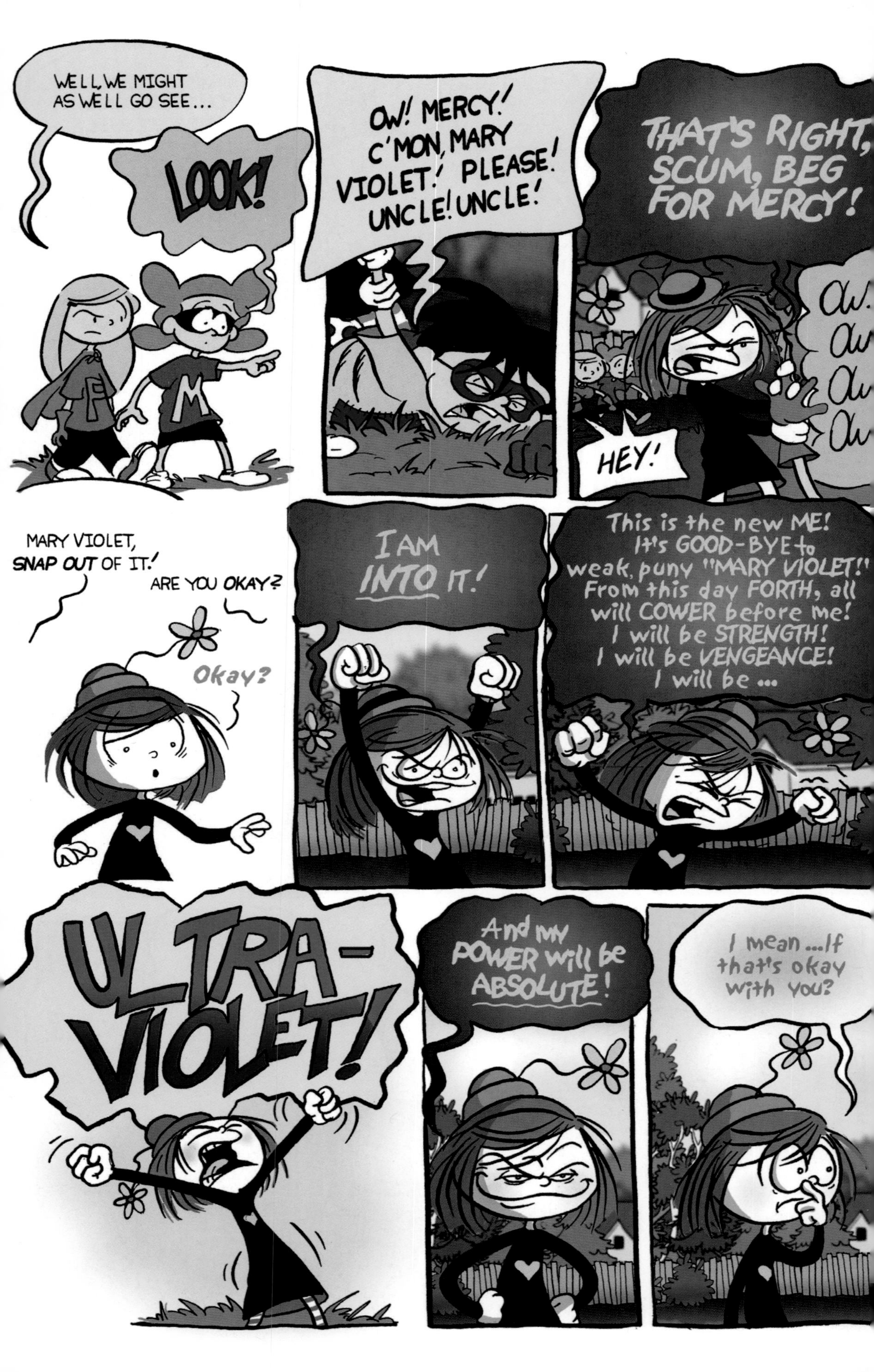

WELL, WE MIGHT AS WELL GO SEE...
LOOK!
OW! MERCY! C'MON, MARY VIOLET! PLEASE! UNCLE! UNCLE!
THAT'S RIGHT, SCUM, BEG FOR MERCY!
HEY!
MARY VIOLET, SNAP OUT OF IT!
ARE YOU OKAY?
Okay?
I AM INTO IT!
This is the new ME! It's GOOD-BYE to weak, puny "MARY VIOLET!" From this day FORTH, all will COWER before me! I will be STRENGTH! I will be VENGEANCE! I will be ...
ULTRA-VIOLET!
And my POWER will be ABSOLUTE!
I mean ...If that's okay with you?

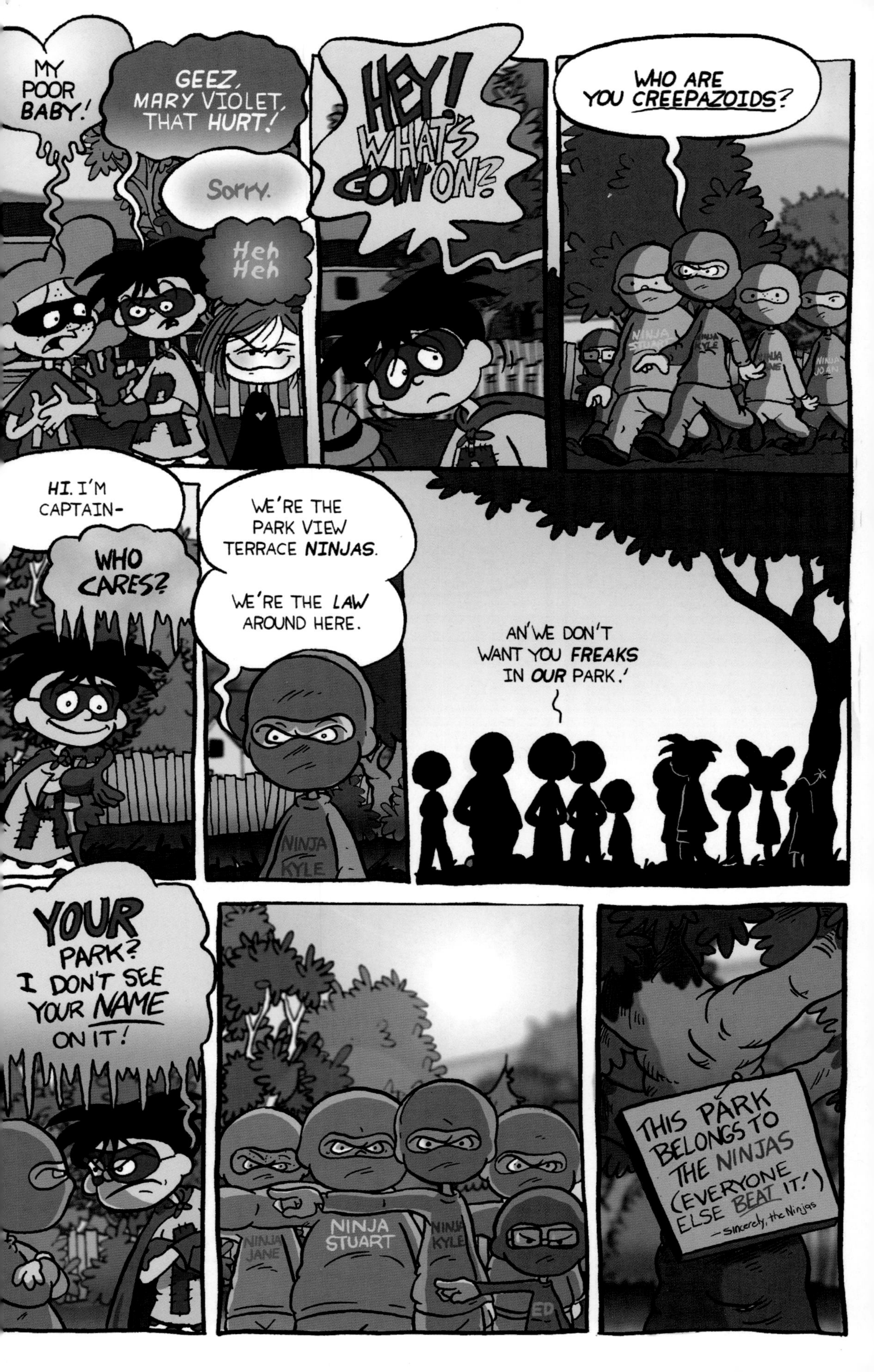
MY POOR BABY!
GEEZ, MARY VIOLET, THAT HURT!
Sorry.
Heh Heh
HEY! WHAT'S GOIN' ON?
WHO ARE YOU CREEPAZOIDS?
NINJA STUART
NINJA KYLE
NINJA JOAN
HI. I'M CAPTAIN-
WHO CARES?
WE'RE THE PARK VIEW TERRACE NINJAS.
WE'RE THE LAW AROUND HERE.
NINJA KYLE
AN' WE DON'T WANT YOU FREAKS IN OUR PARK.'
YOUR PARK? I DON'T SEE YOUR NAME ON IT!
NINJA JANE
NINJA STUART
NINJA KYLE
THIS PARK BELONGS TO THE NINJAS (EVERYONE ELSE BEAT IT!)
—sincerely, the Ninjas

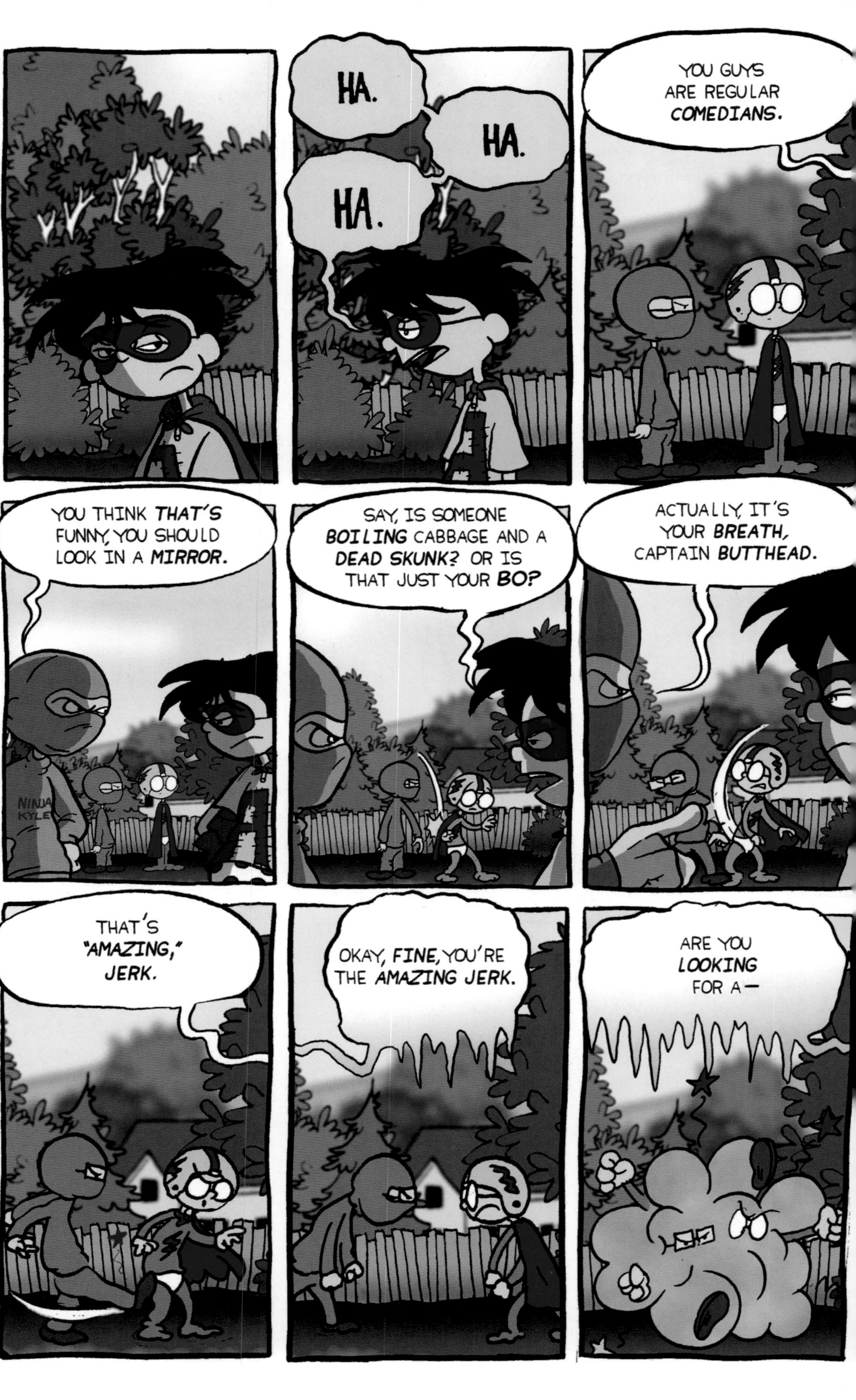
HA.
HA.
HA.
YOU GUYS ARE REGULAR **COMEDIANS.**
YOU THINK **THAT'S** FUNNY, YOU SHOULD LOOK IN A **MIRROR.**
NINJA KYLE
SAY, IS SOMEONE **BOILING** CABBAGE AND A **DEAD SKUNK?** OR IS THAT JUST YOUR **BO?**
ACTUALLY, IT'S YOUR **BREATH,** CAPTAIN **BUTTHEAD.**
THAT'S **"AMAZING,"** **JERK.**
OKAY, **FINE,** YOU'RE THE **AMAZING JERK.**
ARE YOU **LOOKING** FOR A—

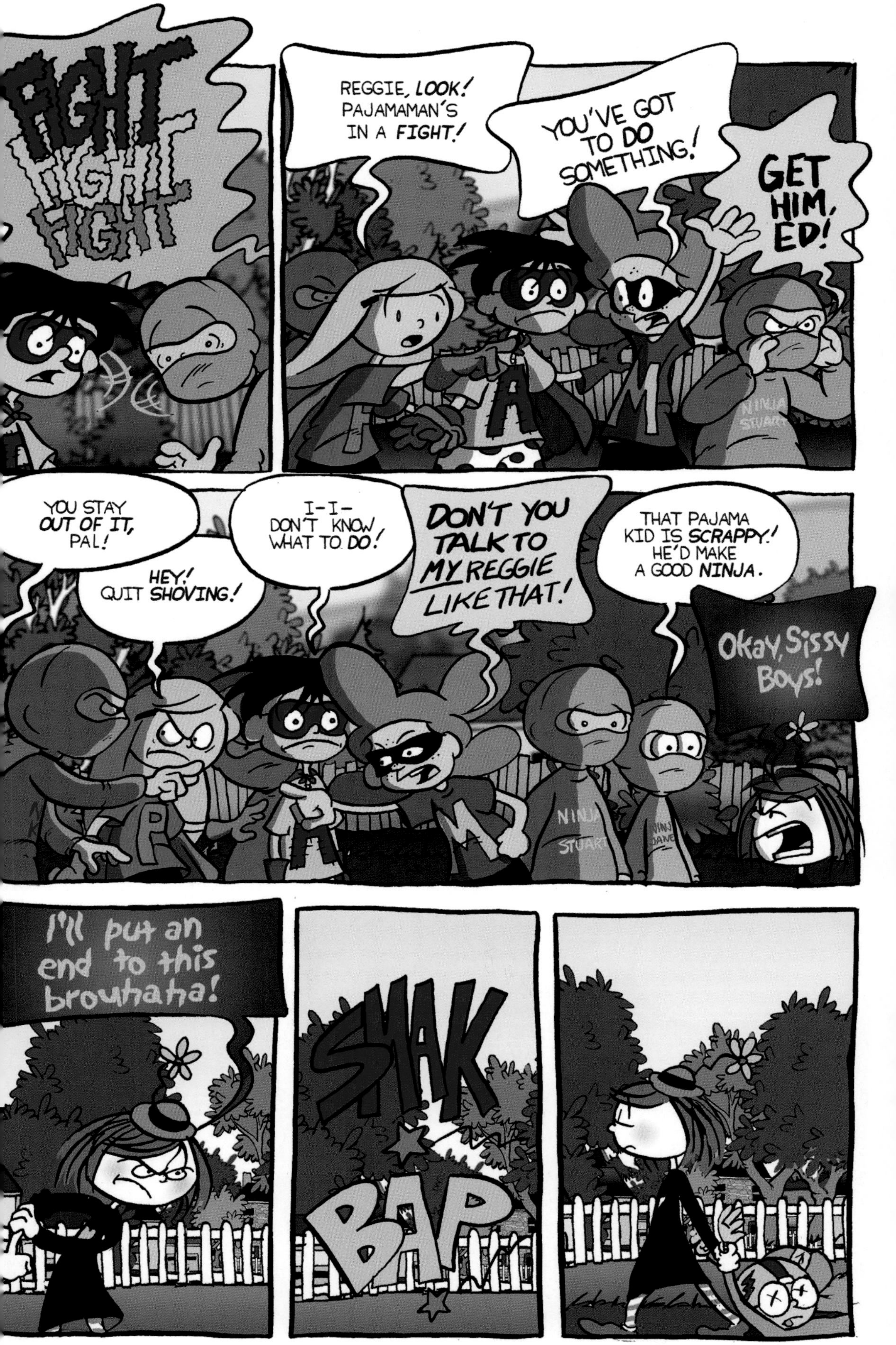

FIGHT FIGHT FIGHT
REGGIE, LOOK! PAJAMAMAN'S IN A FIGHT!
YOU'VE GOT TO DO SOMETHING!
GET HIM, ED!
NINJA STUART
YOU STAY OUT OF IT, PAL!
HEY! QUIT SHOVING!
I-I- DON'T KNOW WHAT TO DO!
DON'T YOU TALK TO MY REGGIE LIKE THAT!
THAT PAJAMA KID IS SCRAPPY! HE'D MAKE A GOOD NINJA.
Okay, Sissy Boys!
NINJA STUART
I'll put an end to this brouhaha!
SMAK
BAP

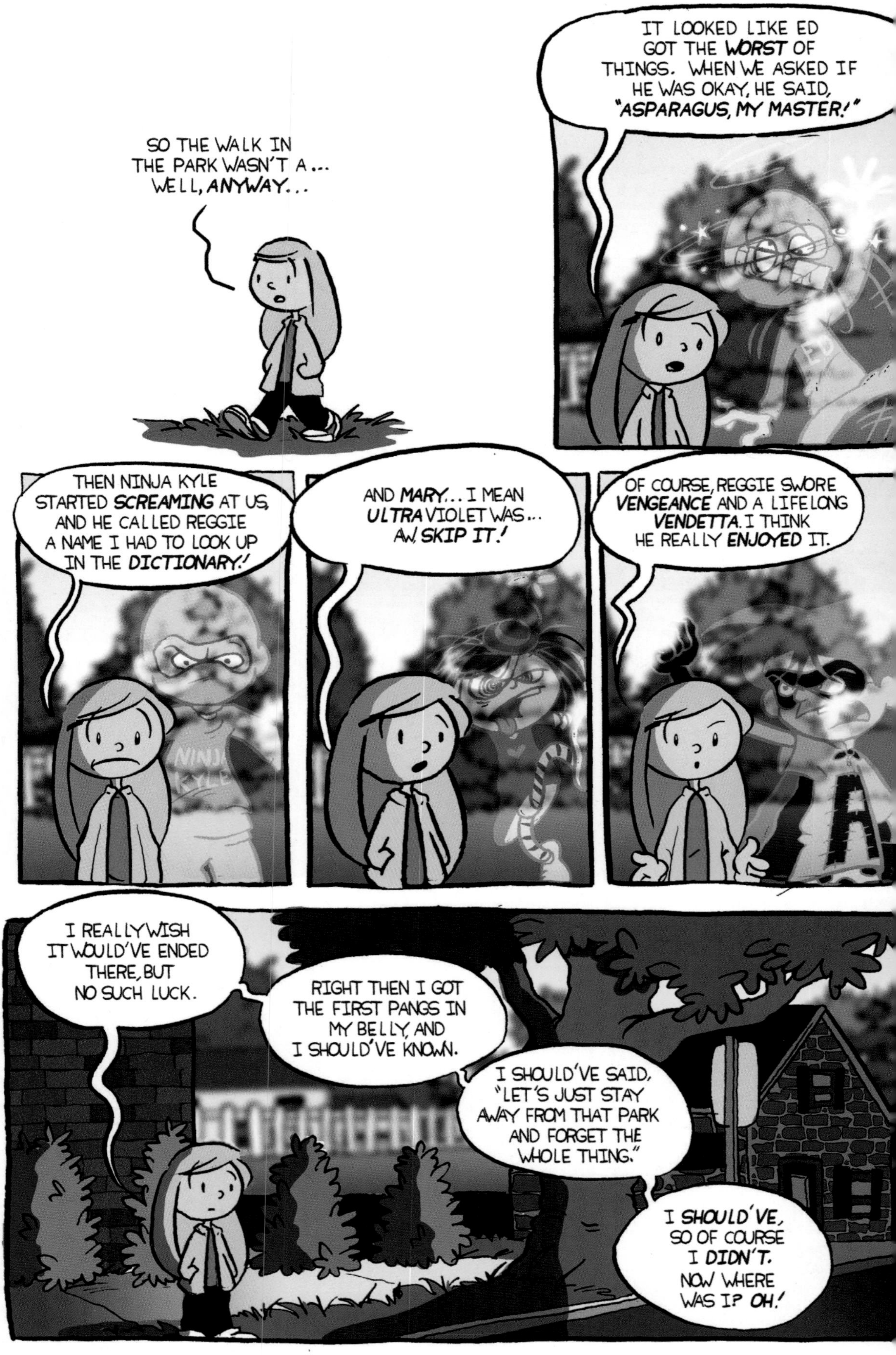

SO THE WALK IN THE PARK WASN'T A... WELL, ANYWAY...
IT LOOKED LIKE ED GOT THE WORST OF THINGS. WHEN WE ASKED IF HE WAS OKAY, HE SAID, "ASPARAGUS, MY MASTER!"
ED
THEN NINJA KYLE STARTED SCREAMING AT US, AND HE CALLED REGGIE A NAME I HAD TO LOOK UP IN THE DICTIONARY!
NINJA KYLE
AND MARY... I MEAN ULTRAVIOLET WAS... AW, SKIP IT!
OF COURSE, REGGIE SWORE VENGEANCE AND A LIFELONG VENDETTA. I THINK HE REALLY ENJOYED IT.
I REALLY WISH IT WOULD'VE ENDED THERE, BUT NO SUCH LUCK.
RIGHT THEN I GOT THE FIRST PANGS IN MY BELLY, AND I SHOULD'VE KNOWN.
I SHOULD'VE SAID, "LET'S JUST STAY AWAY FROM THAT PARK AND FORGET THE WHOLE THING."
I SHOULD'VE, SO OF COURSE I DIDN'T. NOW WHERE WAS I? OH!

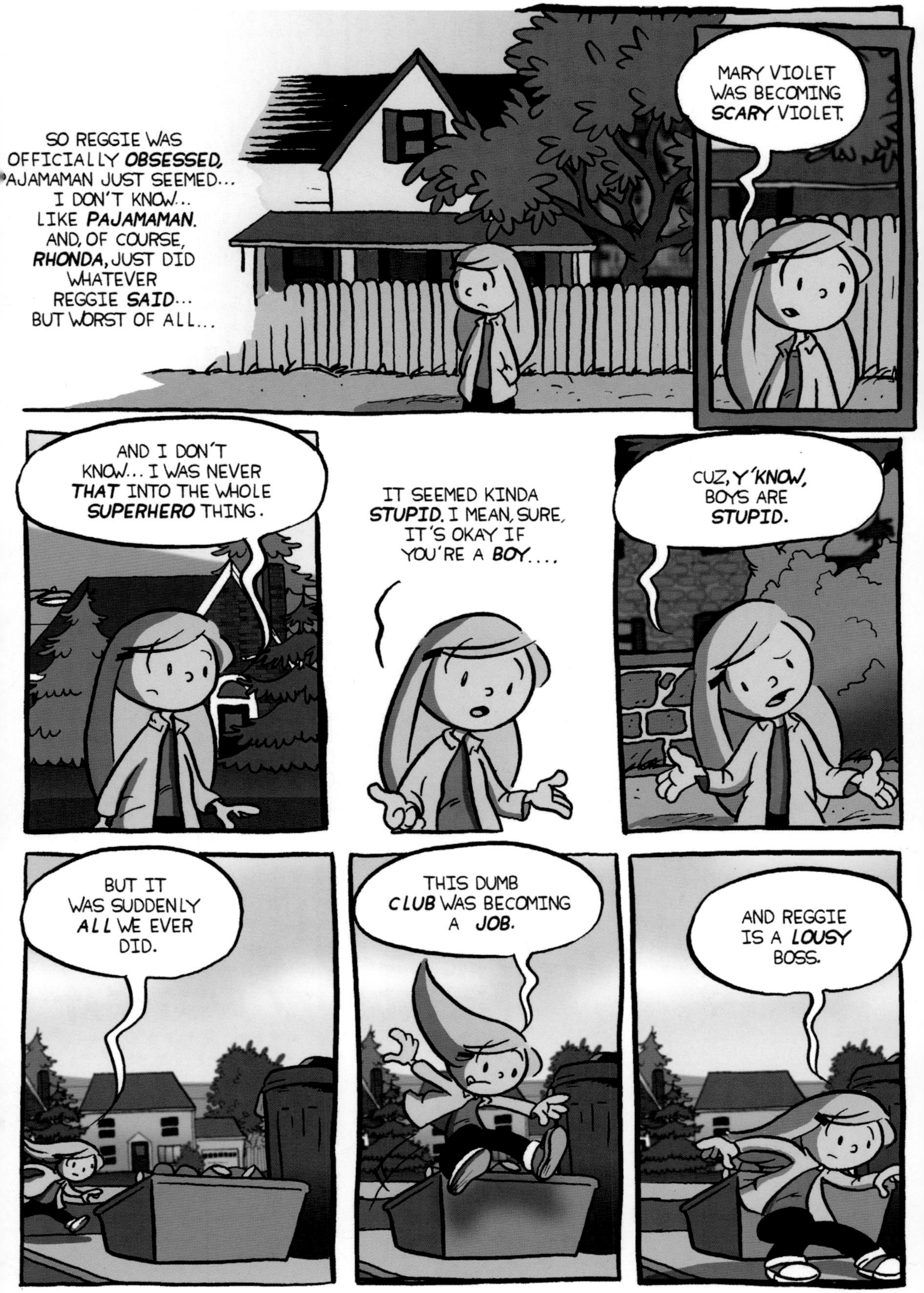
SO REGGIE WAS OFFICIALLY OBSESSED, PAJAMAMAN JUST SEEMED... I DON'T KNOW... LIKE PAJAMAMAN. AND, OF COURSE, RHONDA, JUST DID WHATEVER REGGIE SAID... BUT WORST OF ALL...
MARY VIOLET WAS BECOMING SCARY VIOLET.
AND I DON'T KNOW... I WAS NEVER THAT INTO THE WHOLE SUPERHERO THING.
IT SEEMED KINDA STUPID. I MEAN, SURE, IT'S OKAY IF YOU'RE A BOY....
CUZ, Y'KNOW, BOYS ARE STUPID.
BUT IT WAS SUDDENLY ALL WE EVER DID.
THIS DUMB CLUB WAS BECOMING A JOB.
AND REGGIE IS A LOUSY BOSS.

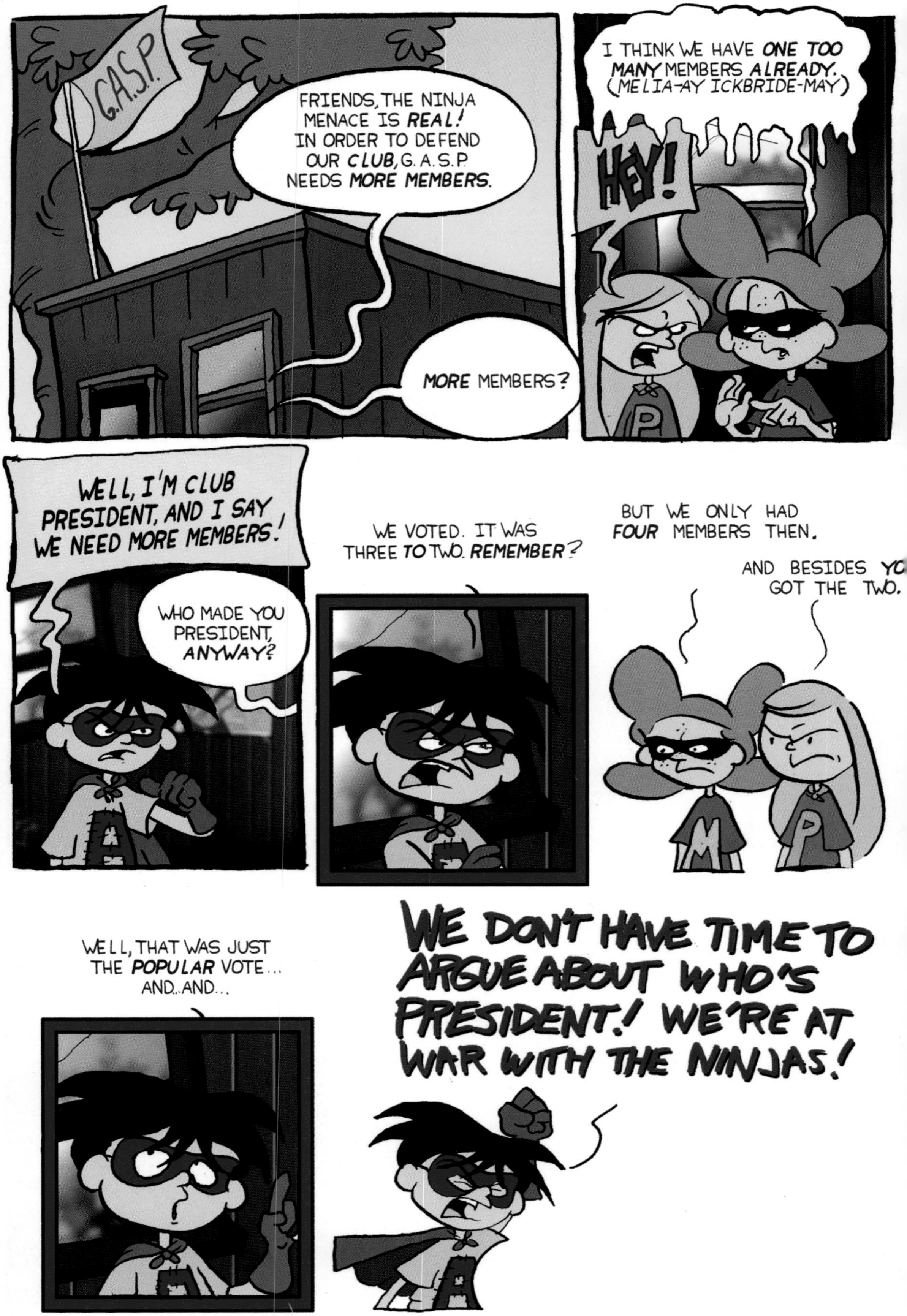

G.A.S.P.
FRIENDS, THE NINJA MENACE IS REAL! IN ORDER TO DEFEND OUR CLUB, G.A.S.P. NEEDS MORE MEMBERS.
MORE MEMBERS?
HEY!
I THINK WE HAVE ONE TOO MANY MEMBERS ALREADY. (MELIA-AY ICKBRIDE-MAY)
WELL, I'M CLUB PRESIDENT, AND I SAY WE NEED MORE MEMBERS!
WHO MADE YOU PRESIDENT, ANYWAY?
WE VOTED. IT WAS THREE TO TWO. REMEMBER?
BUT WE ONLY HAD FOUR MEMBERS THEN.
AND BESIDES YO GOT THE TWO.
WELL, THAT WAS JUST THE POPULAR VOTE... AND..AND...
WE DON'T HAVE TIME TO ARGUE ABOUT WHO'S PRESIDENT! WE'RE AT WAR WITH THE NINJAS!

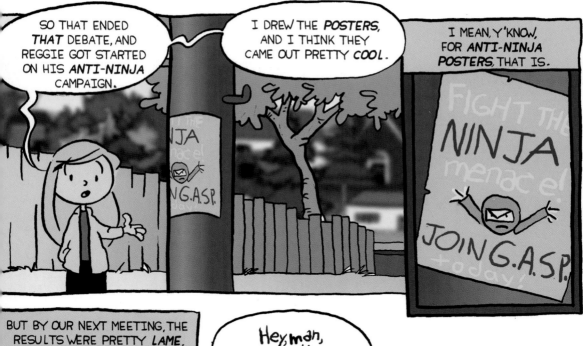

SO THAT ENDED *THAT* DEBATE, AND REGGIE GOT STARTED ON HIS *ANTI-NINJA* CAMPAIGN.

I DREW THE *POSTERS*, AND I THINK THEY CAME OUT PRETTY *COOL*.

I MEAN, Y'KNOW, FOR *ANTI-NINJA POSTERS*, THAT IS.

FIGHT THE NINJA menace! JOIN G.A.S.P. today!

BUT BY OUR NEXT MEETING, THE RESULTS WERE PRETTY *LAME*.

THIS IS IT?

Hey, man, how's it goin'?

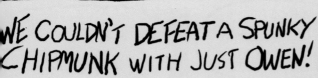

WE COULDN'T DEFEAT A SPUNKY CHIPMUNK WITH JUST OWEN!

May I give him the Trials?

ULTRAVIOLET, PLEASE DON'T BREAK OUR *ONLY RECRUIT*.

Spunky Chipmunk? What kinda club IS this?

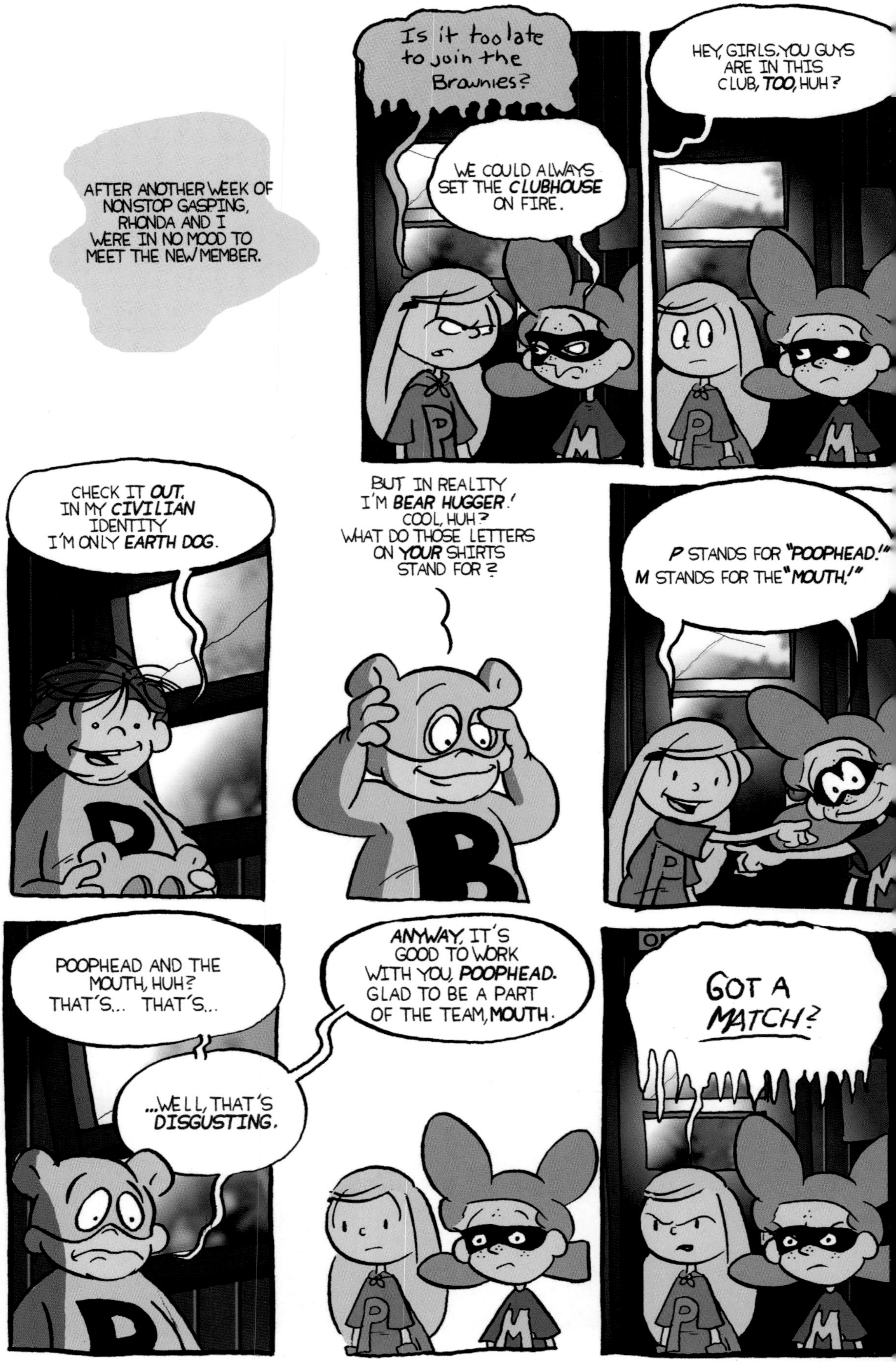

AFTER ANOTHER WEEK OF NONSTOP GASPING, RHONDA AND I WERE IN NO MOOD TO MEET THE NEW MEMBER.
Is it too late to join the Brownies?
WE COULD ALWAYS SET THE CLUBHOUSE ON FIRE.
HEY, GIRLS, YOU GUYS ARE IN THIS CLUB, TOO, HUH?
CHECK IT OUT. IN MY CIVILIAN IDENTITY I'M ONLY EARTH DOG.
BUT IN REALITY I'M BEAR HUGGER! COOL, HUH? WHAT DO THOSE LETTERS ON YOUR SHIRTS STAND FOR?
P STANDS FOR "POOPHEAD!" M STANDS FOR THE "MOUTH!"
POOPHEAD AND THE MOUTH, HUH? THAT'S... THAT'S...
...WELL, THAT'S DISGUSTING.
ANYWAY, IT'S GOOD TO WORK WITH YOU, POOPHEAD. GLAD TO BE A PART OF THE TEAM, MOUTH.
GOT A MATCH?

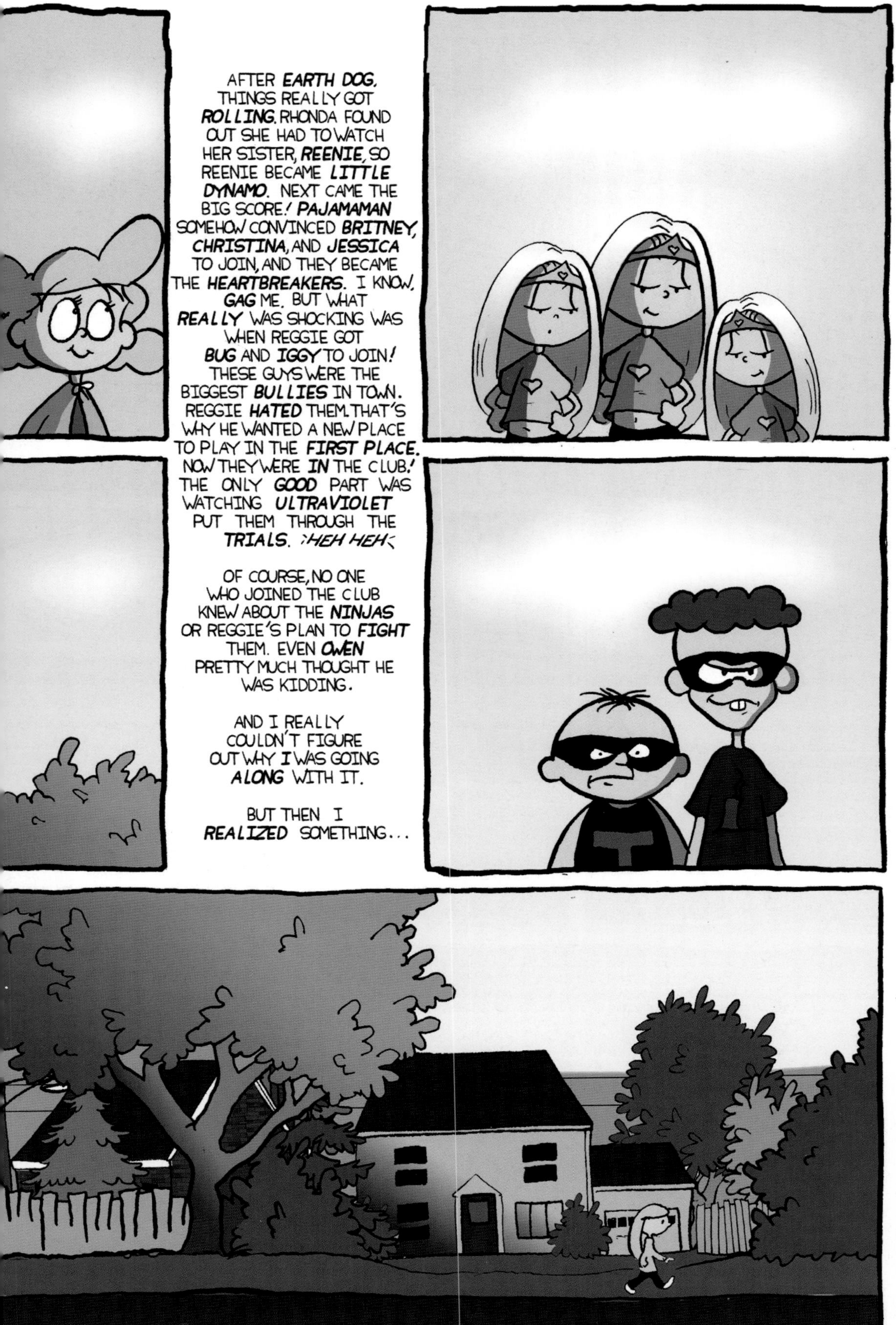
AFTER EARTH DOG, THINGS REALLY GOT ROLLING. RHONDA FOUND OUT SHE HAD TO WATCH HER SISTER, REENIE, SO REENIE BECAME LITTLE DYNAMO. NEXT CAME THE BIG SCORE! PAJAMAMAN SOMEHOW CONVINCED BRITNEY, CHRISTINA, AND JESSICA TO JOIN, AND THEY BECAME THE HEARTBREAKERS. I KNOW, GAG ME. BUT WHAT REALLY WAS SHOCKING WAS WHEN REGGIE GOT BUG AND IGGY TO JOIN! THESE GUYS WERE THE BIGGEST BULLIES IN TOWN. REGGIE HATED THEM. THAT'S WHY HE WANTED A NEW PLACE TO PLAY IN THE FIRST PLACE. NOW THEY WERE IN THE CLUB! THE ONLY GOOD PART WAS WATCHING ULTRAVIOLET PUT THEM THROUGH THE TRIALS. >HEH HEH<
OF COURSE, NO ONE WHO JOINED THE CLUB KNEW ABOUT THE NINJAS OR REGGIE'S PLAN TO FIGHT THEM. EVEN OWEN PRETTY MUCH THOUGHT HE WAS KIDDING.
AND I REALLY COULDN'T FIGURE OUT WHY I WAS GOING ALONG WITH IT.
BUT THEN I REALIZED SOMETHING...

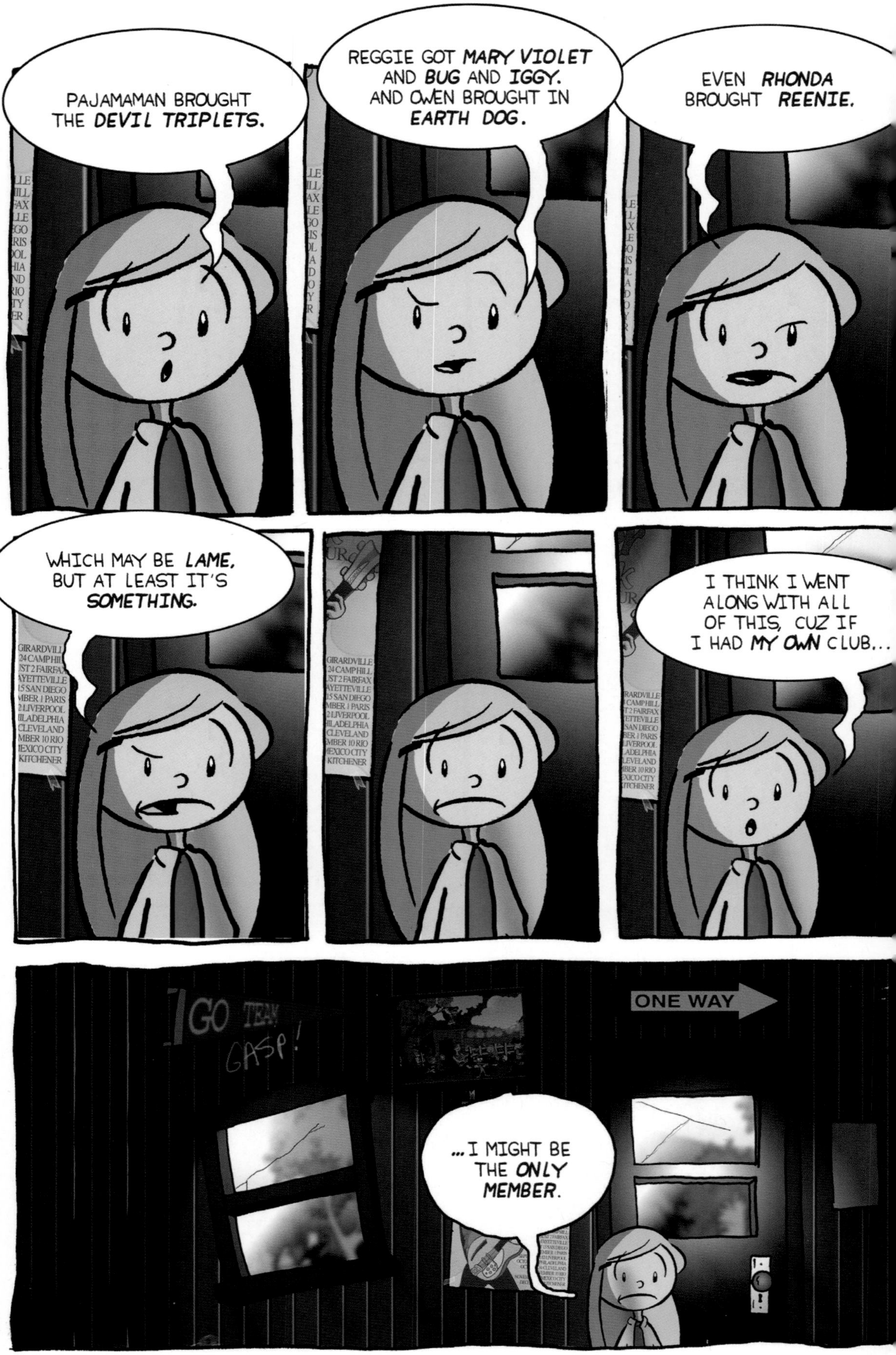
PAJAMAMAN BROUGHT THE DEVIL TRIPLETS.
REGGIE GOT MARY VIOLET AND BUG AND IGGY. AND OWEN BROUGHT IN EARTH DOG.
EVEN RHONDA BROUGHT REENIE.
WHICH MAY BE LAME, BUT AT LEAST IT'S SOMETHING.
I THINK I WENT ALONG WITH ALL OF THIS, CUZ IF I HAD MY OWN CLUB...
GIRARDVILLE
24 CAMP HILL
UST 2 FAIRFAX
AYETTEVILLE
15 SAN DIEGO
MBER 1 PARIS
2 LIVERPOOL
HILADELPHIA
CLEVELAND
MBER 10 RIO
MEXICO CITY
KITCHENER
GO TEAM
GASP!
ONE WAY
...I MIGHT BE THE ONLY MEMBER.

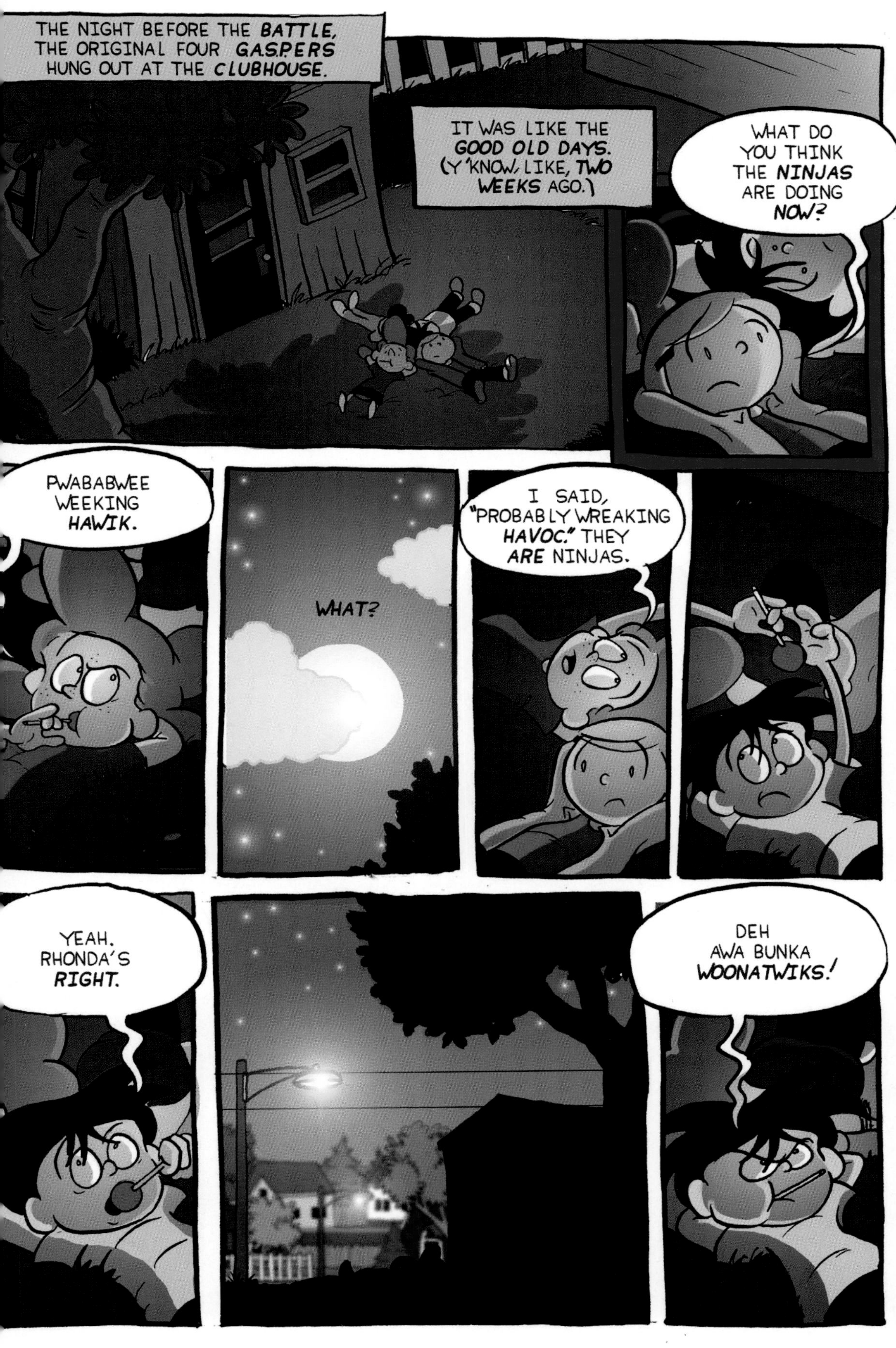
THE NIGHT BEFORE THE BATTLE, THE ORIGINAL FOUR GAS.P.ERS HUNG OUT AT THE CLUBHOUSE.
IT WAS LIKE THE GOOD OLD DAYS. (Y'KNOW, LIKE, TWO WEEKS AGO.)
WHAT DO YOU THINK THE NINJAS ARE DOING NOW?
PWABABWEE WEEKING HAWIK.
WHAT?
I SAID, "PROBABLY WREAKING HAVOC." THEY ARE NINJAS.
YEAH. RHONDA'S RIGHT.
DEH AWA BUNKA WOONATWIKS!

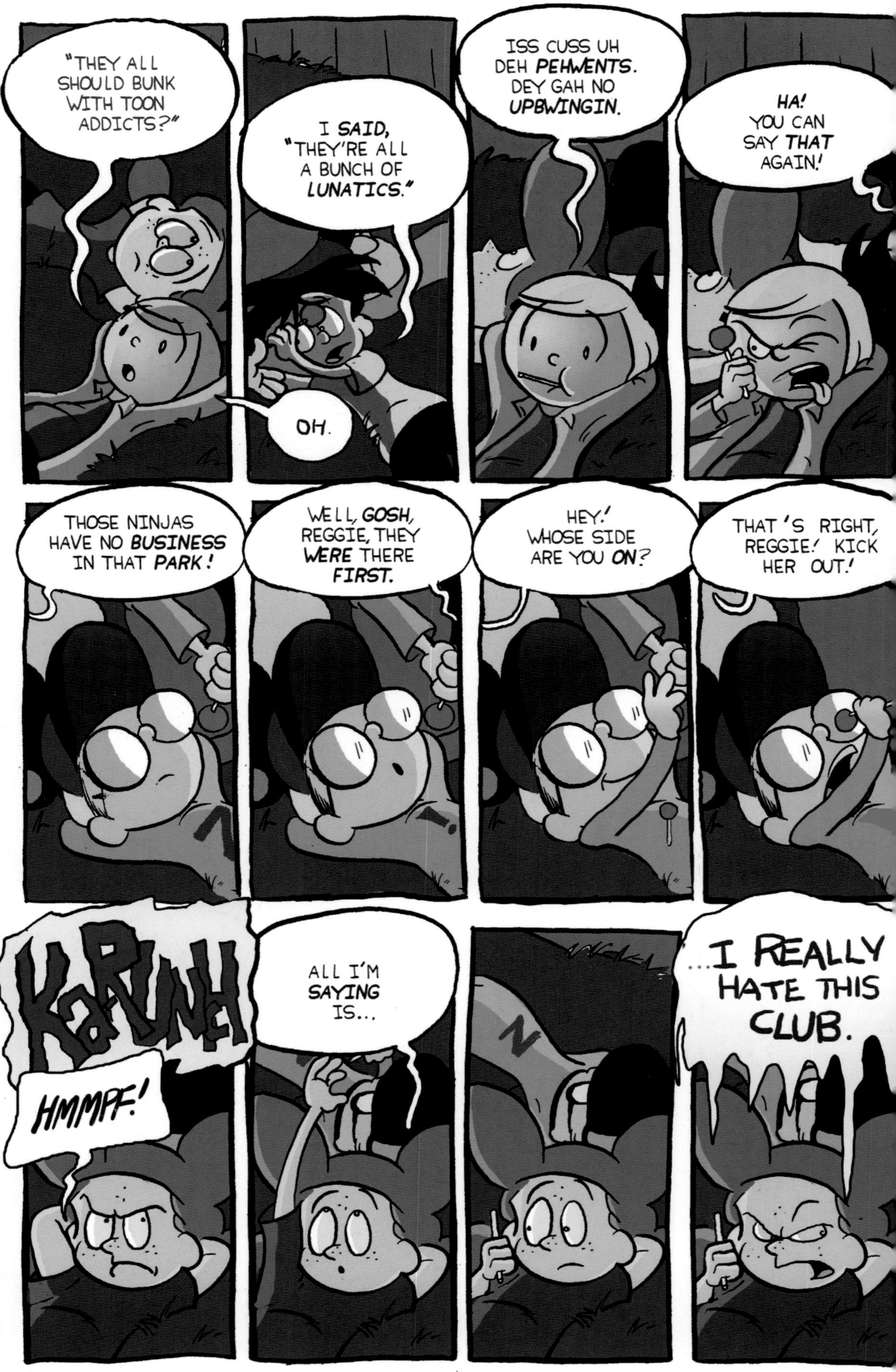
"THEY ALL SHOULD BUNK WITH TOON ADDICTS?"
I SAID, "THEY'RE ALL A BUNCH OF LUNATICS."
OH.
ISS CUSS UH DEH PEHWENTS. DEY GAH NO UPBWINGIN.
HA! YOU CAN SAY THAT AGAIN!
THOSE NINJAS HAVE NO BUSINESS IN THAT PARK!
WELL, GOSH, REGGIE, THEY WERE THERE FIRST.
HEY! WHOSE SIDE ARE YOU ON?
THAT'S RIGHT, REGGIE! KICK HER OUT!
KaRUNCH
HMMPF!
ALL I'M SAYING IS...
...I REALLY HATE THIS CLUB.

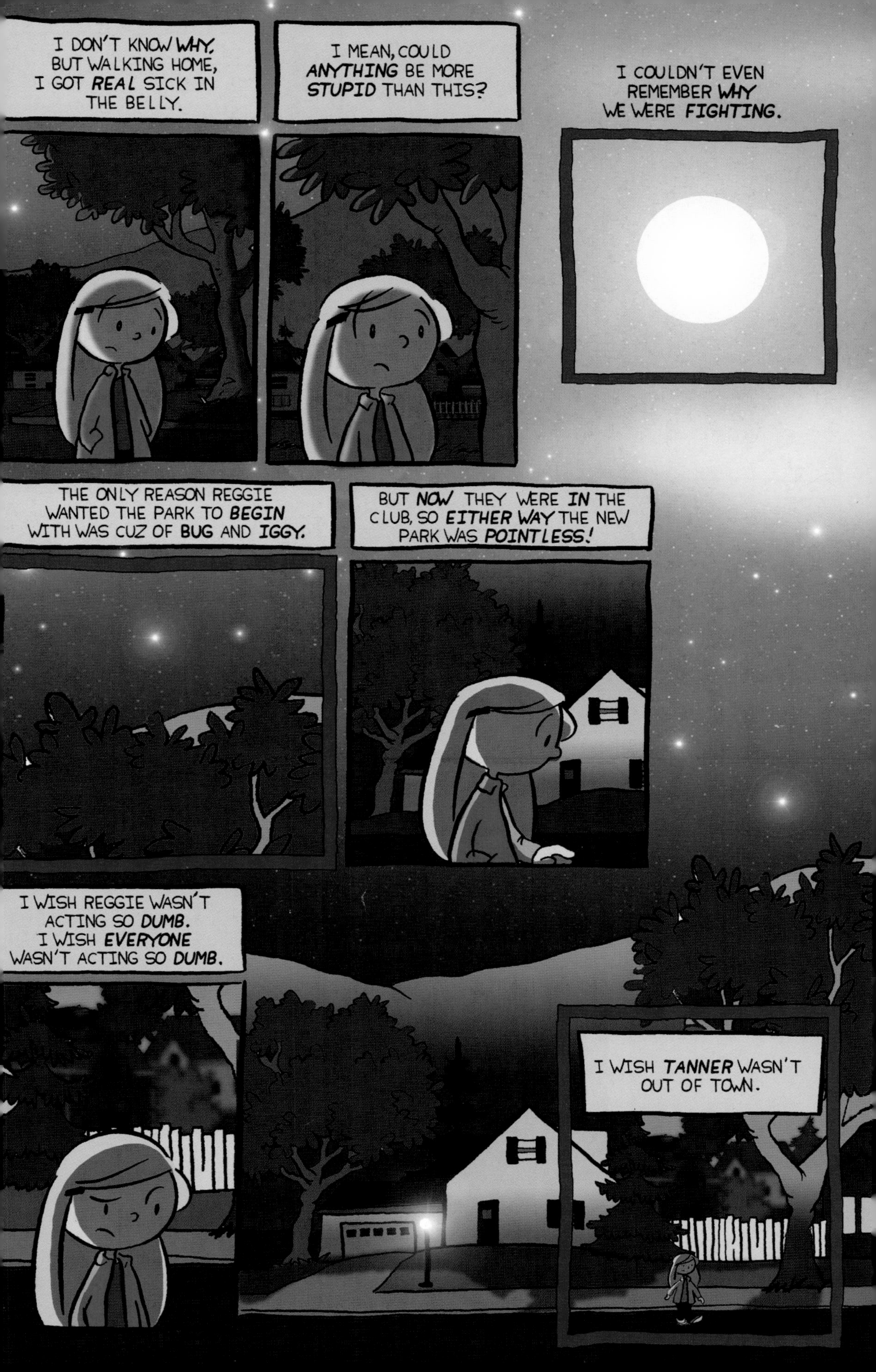
I DON'T KNOW WHY. BUT WALKING HOME, I GOT REAL SICK IN THE BELLY.
I MEAN, COULD ANYTHING BE MORE STUPID THAN THIS?
I COULDN'T EVEN REMEMBER WHY WE WERE FIGHTING.
THE ONLY REASON REGGIE WANTED THE PARK TO BEGIN WITH WAS CUZ OF BUG AND IGGY.
BUT NOW THEY WERE IN THE CLUB, SO EITHER WAY THE NEW PARK WAS POINTLESS!
I WISH REGGIE WASN'T ACTING SO DUMB. I WISH EVERYONE WASN'T ACTING SO DUMB.
I WISH TANNER WASN'T OUT OF TOWN.

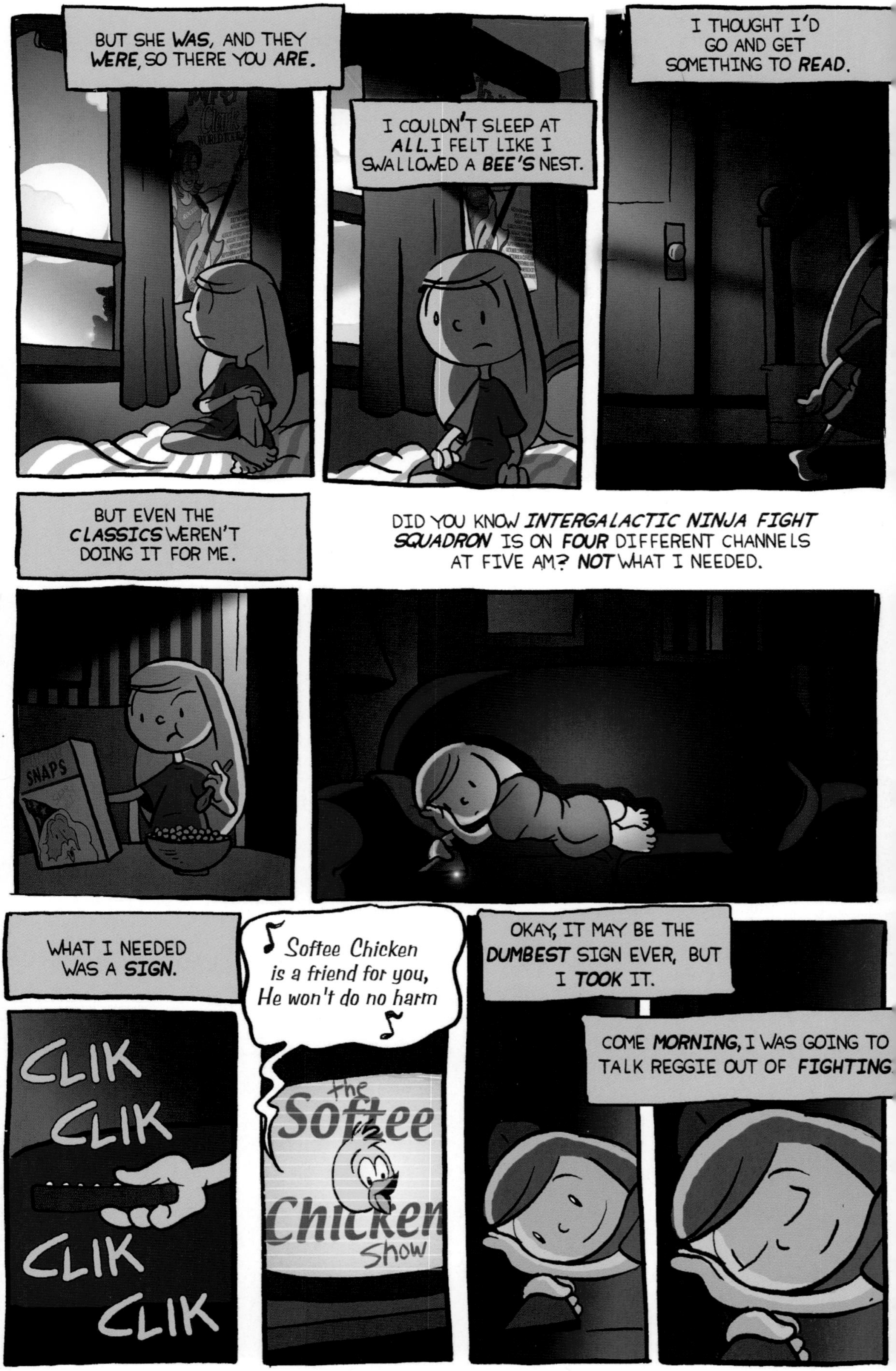

BUT SHE WAS, AND THEY WERE, SO THERE YOU ARE.
I COULDN'T SLEEP AT ALL. I FELT LIKE I SWALLOWED A BEE'S NEST.
I THOUGHT I'D GO AND GET SOMETHING TO READ.
BUT EVEN THE CLASSICS WEREN'T DOING IT FOR ME.
DID YOU KNOW INTERGALACTIC NINJA FIGHT SQUADRON IS ON FOUR DIFFERENT CHANNELS AT FIVE AM? NOT WHAT I NEEDED.
SNAPS
WHAT I NEEDED WAS A SIGN.
CLIK CLIK
CLIK CLIK
Softee Chicken is a friend for you, He won't do no harm
the Softee Chicken show
OKAY, IT MAY BE THE DUMBEST SIGN EVER, BUT I TOOK IT.
COME MORNING, I WAS GOING TO TALK REGGIE OUT OF FIGHTING.

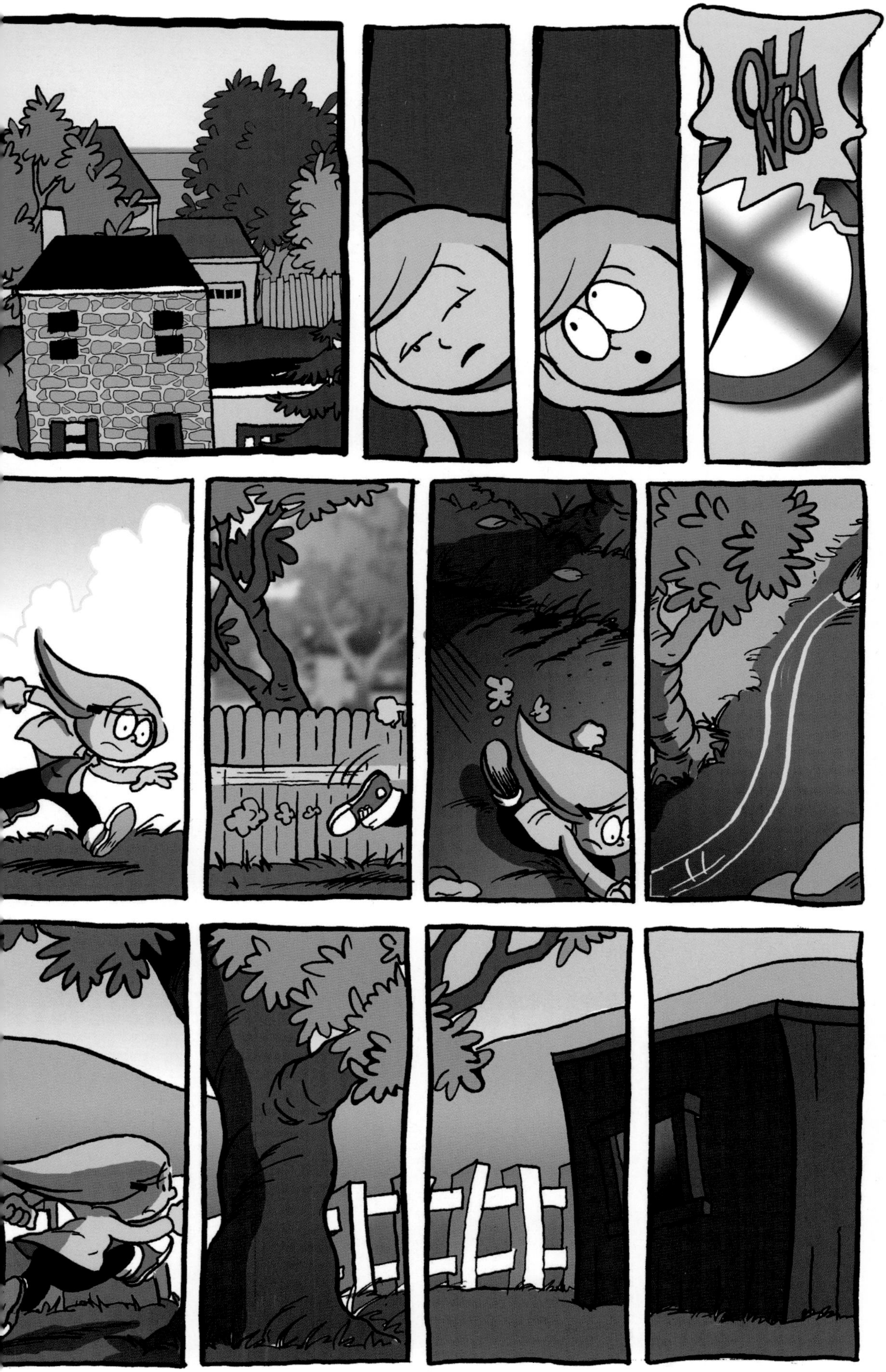
OH NO!

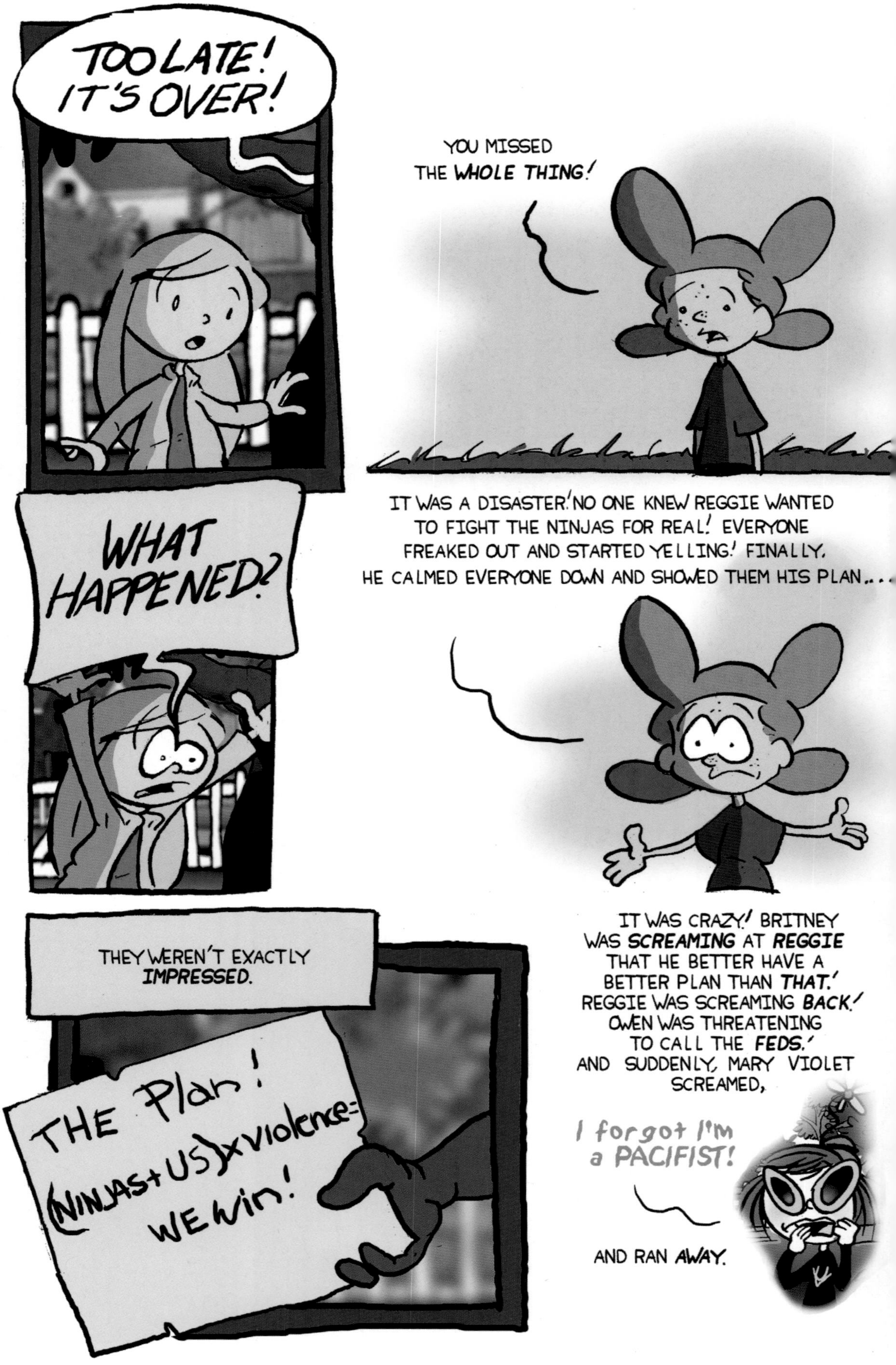
TOO LATE! IT'S OVER!
YOU MISSED THE WHOLE THING!
WHAT HAPPENED?
IT WAS A DISASTER! NO ONE KNEW REGGIE WANTED TO FIGHT THE NINJAS FOR REAL! EVERYONE FREAKED OUT AND STARTED YELLING! FINALLY, HE CALMED EVERYONE DOWN AND SHOWED THEM HIS PLAN....
THEY WEREN'T EXACTLY IMPRESSED.
THE Plan!
(NINJAS+US)xviolence=
WE win!
IT WAS CRAZY! BRITNEY WAS SCREAMING AT REGGIE THAT HE BETTER HAVE A BETTER PLAN THAN THAT! REGGIE WAS SCREAMING BACK! OWEN WAS THREATENING TO CALL THE FEDS! AND SUDDENLY, MARY VIOLET SCREAMED,
I forgot I'm a PACIFIST!
AND RAN AWAY.

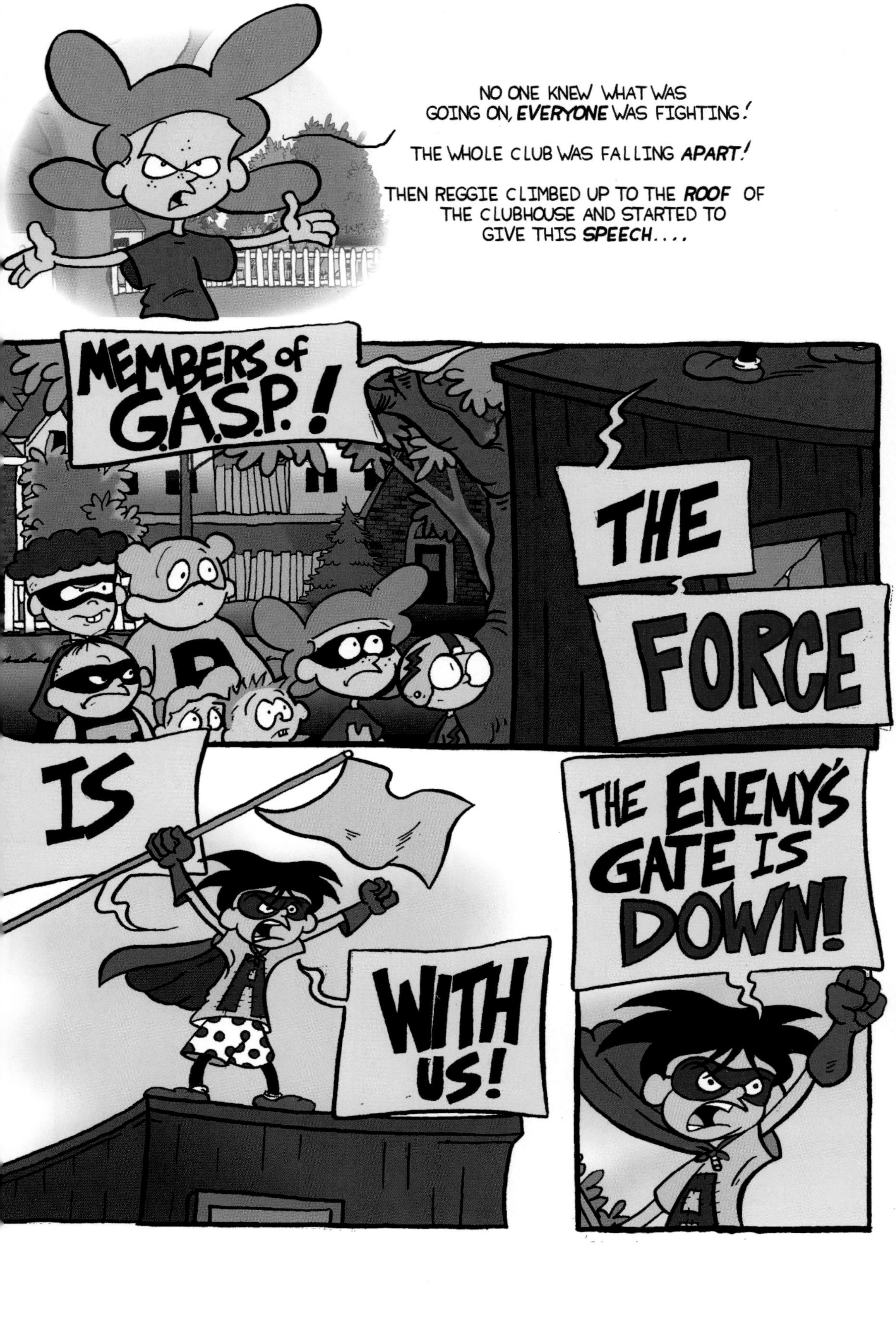
NO ONE KNEW WHAT WAS GOING ON, EVERYONE WAS FIGHTING!
THE WHOLE CLUB WAS FALLING APART!
THEN REGGIE CLIMBED UP TO THE ROOF OF THE CLUBHOUSE AND STARTED TO GIVE THIS SPEECH....
MEMBERS of G.A.S.P.!
THE
FORCE
IS
WITH US!
THE ENEMY'S GATE IS DOWN!

BUT A SHADOW RISES IN THE **EAST!**

WHICH SEEKS TO BE THE ULTIMATE POWER IN THE UNIVERSE!

BUT BY THE **POWER** OF G.A.S.P., WE HAVE THE **POWER!**

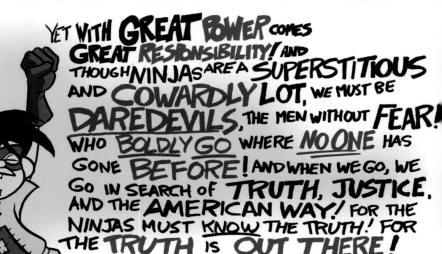

YET WITH **GREAT POWER** COMES **GREAT RESPONSIBILITY!** AND THOUGH NINJAS ARE A **SUPERSTITIOUS** AND **COWARDLY LOT**, WE MUST BE **DAREDEVILS**, THE MEN WITHOUT **FEAR!** WHO **BOLDLY GO** WHERE **NO ONE** HAS GONE **BEFORE!** AND WHEN WE GO, WE GO IN SEARCH OF **TRUTH, JUSTICE**, AND THE **AMERICAN WAY!** FOR THE NINJAS MUST **KNOW** THE TRUTH! FOR THE **TRUTH** IS **OUT THERE!**

MEMBERS OF G.A.S.P., **TODAY** IS **OUR** DAY.

VICTORY IS OUR DESTINY.

AND SO I SAY TO YOU...

WIZZ

THOK!

G.A.S.P.

CHILDREN!

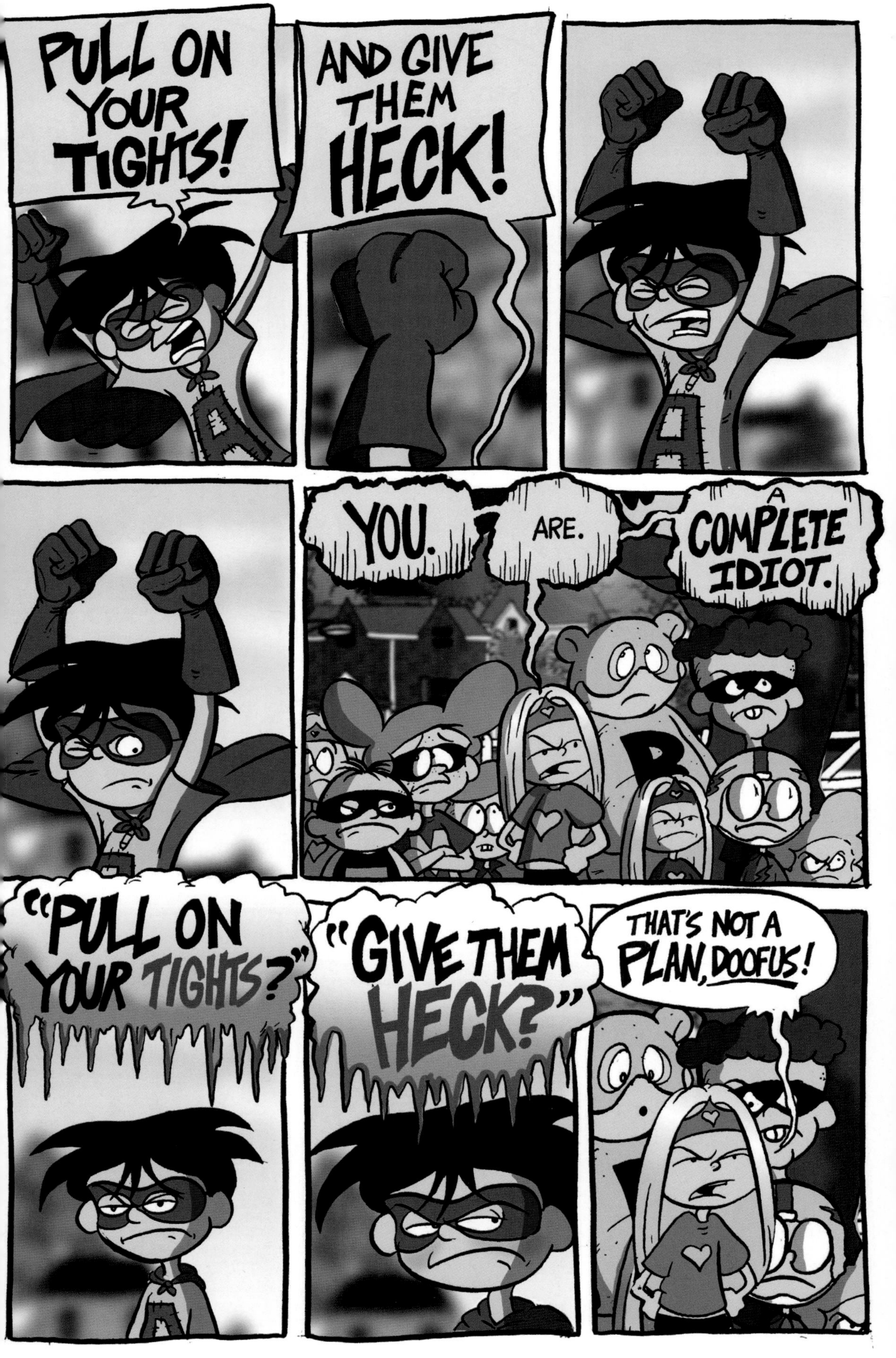
PULL ON YOUR TIGHTS!
AND GIVE THEM HECK!
YOU.
ARE.
A COMPLETE IDIOT.
"PULL ON YOUR TIGHTS?"
"GIVE THEM HECK?"
THAT'S NOT A PLAN, DOOFUS!

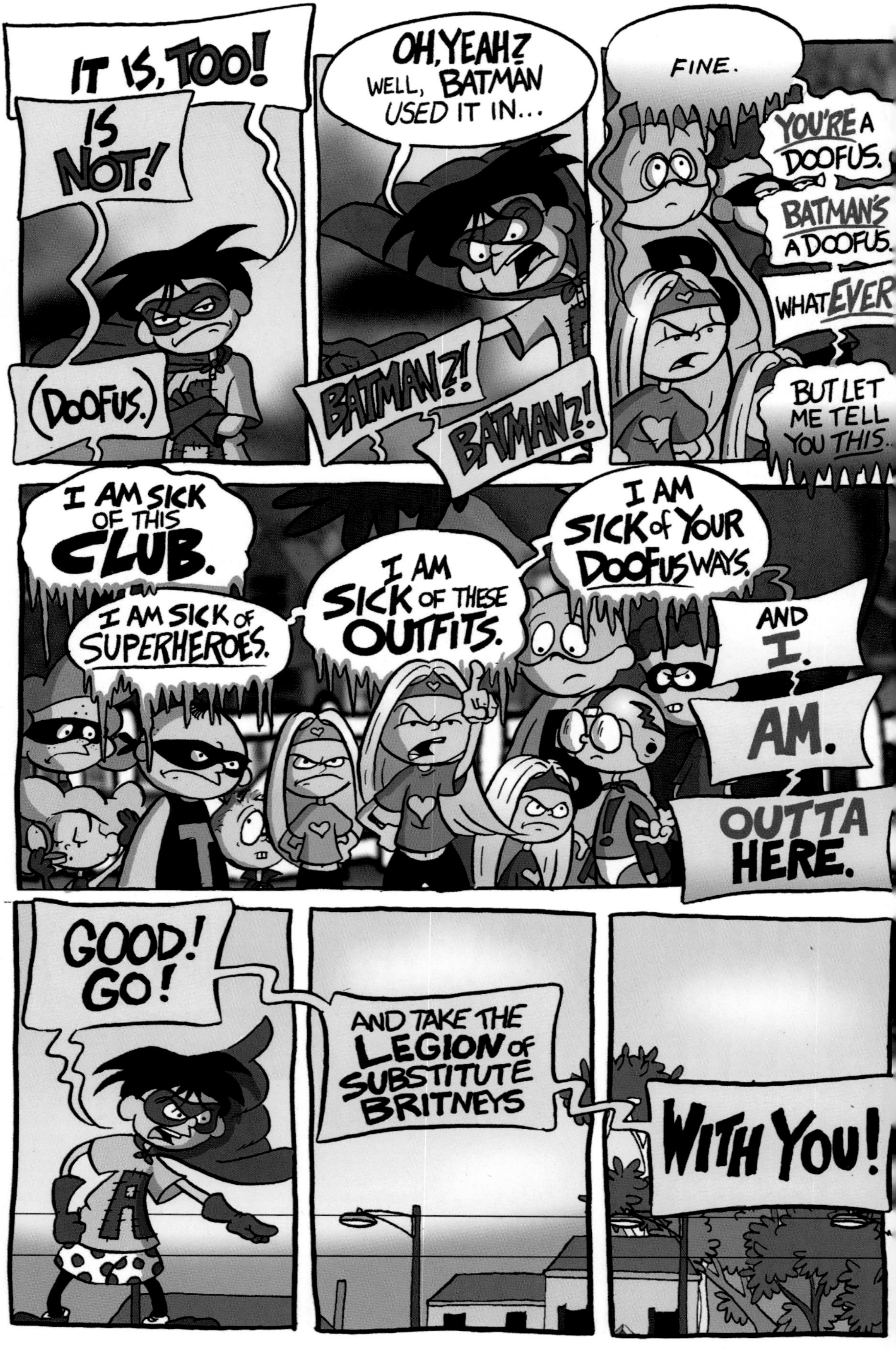
IT IS, TOO!
IS NOT!
(DOOFUS.)
OH, YEAH? WELL, BATMAN USED IT IN...
BATMAN?!
BATMAN?!
FINE.
YOU'RE A DOOFUS.
BATMAN'S A DOOFUS.
WHATEVER
BUT LET ME TELL YOU THIS...
I AM SICK OF THIS CLUB.
I AM SICK OF SUPERHEROES.
I AM SICK OF THESE OUTFITS.
I AM SICK OF YOUR DOOFUS WAYS.
AND I.
AM.
OUTTA HERE.
GOOD! GO!
AND TAKE THE LEGION OF SUBSTITUTE BRITNEYS
WITH YOU!

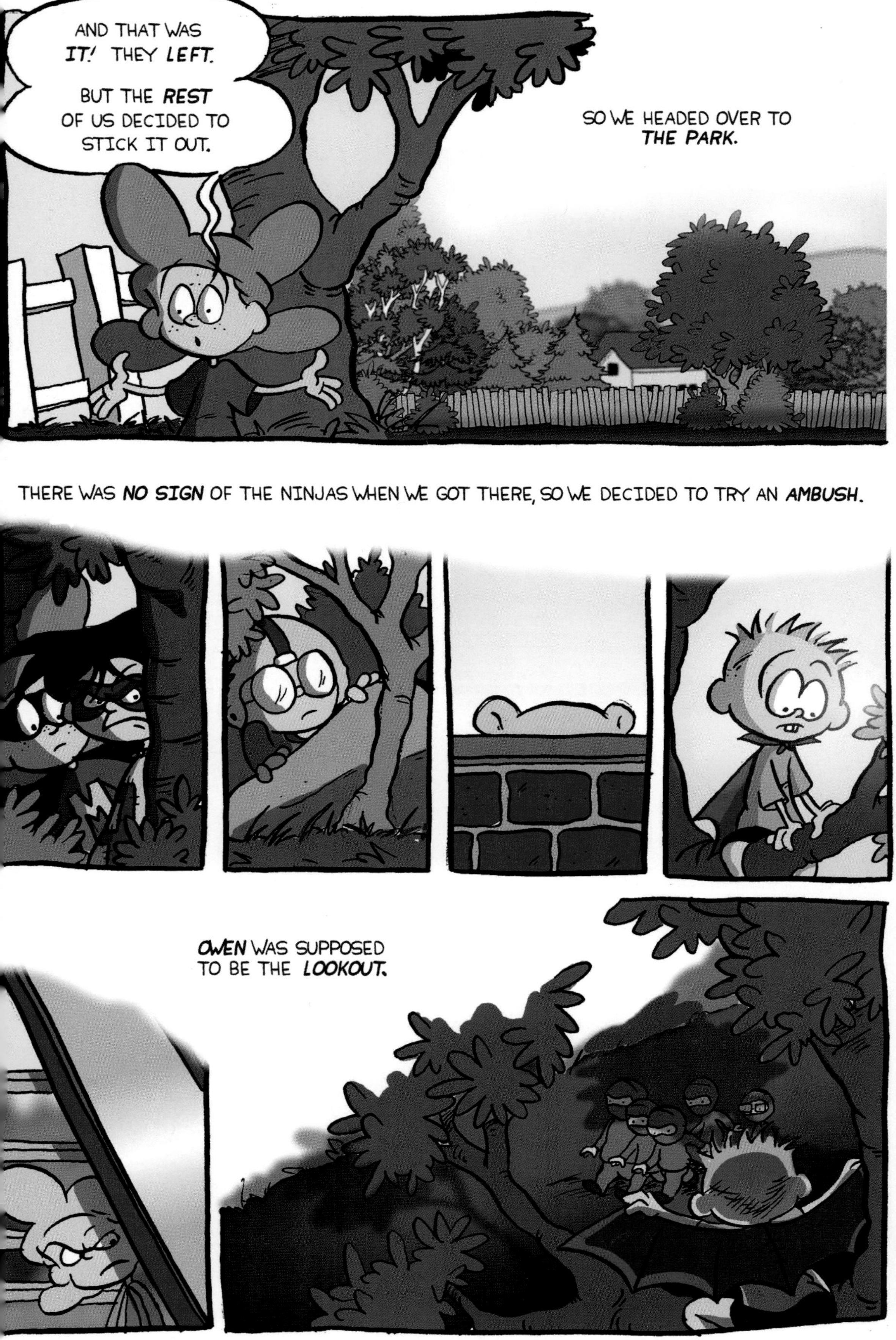
AND THAT WAS IT! THEY LEFT.
BUT THE REST OF US DECIDED TO STICK IT OUT.
SO WE HEADED OVER TO THE PARK.
THERE WAS NO SIGN OF THE NINJAS WHEN WE GOT THERE, SO WE DECIDED TO TRY AN AMBUSH.
OWEN WAS SUPPOSED TO BE THE LOOKOUT.

NO ONE'S REALLY SURE WHAT **HAPPENED.**

MAYBE OWEN DECIDED TO **JUMP.**

MAYBE HE **REALLY THOUGHT** HE COULD **FLY.**

OR MAYBE HE JUST **FELL.**

ALL WE KNOW IS...

...ONE MINUTE HE WAS **IN** THE TREE...

...AND THE **NEXT**...

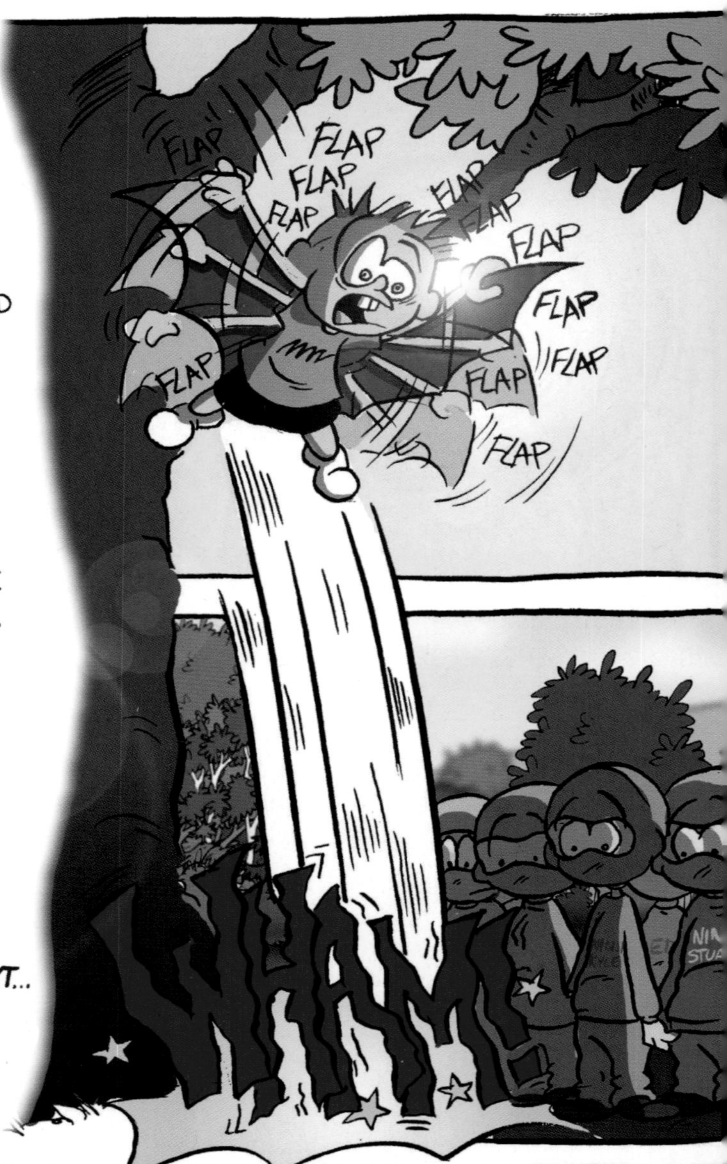
FLAP
FLAP
FLAP
FLAP
FLAP
FLAP
FLAP
FLAP
FLAP
FLAP
FLAP
FLAP
WHAM!

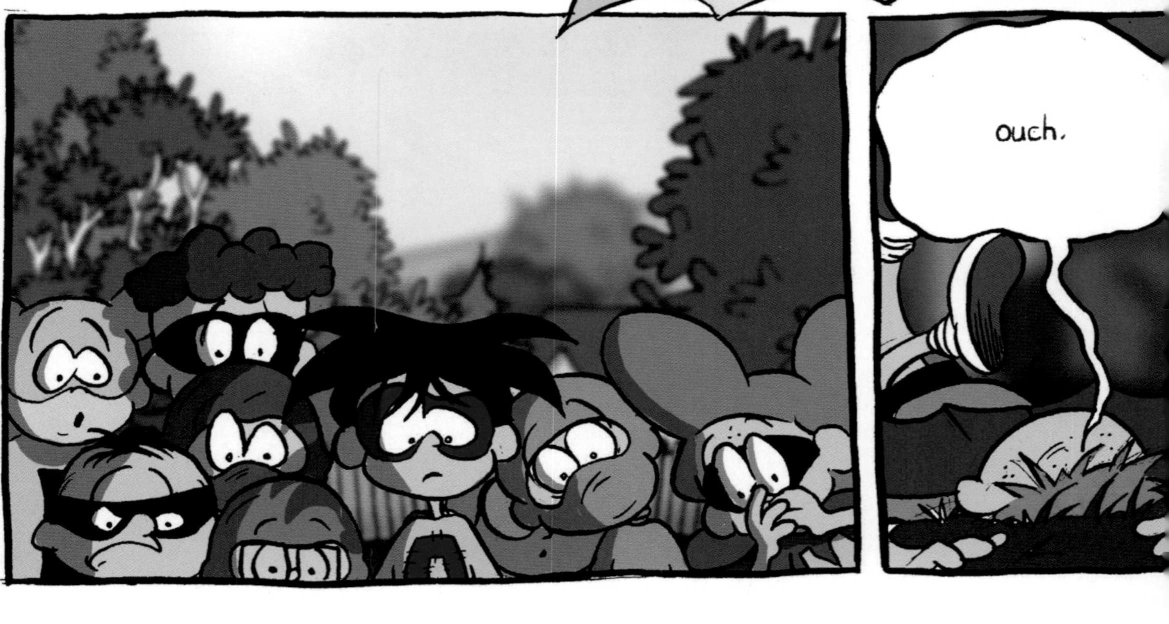
ouch.

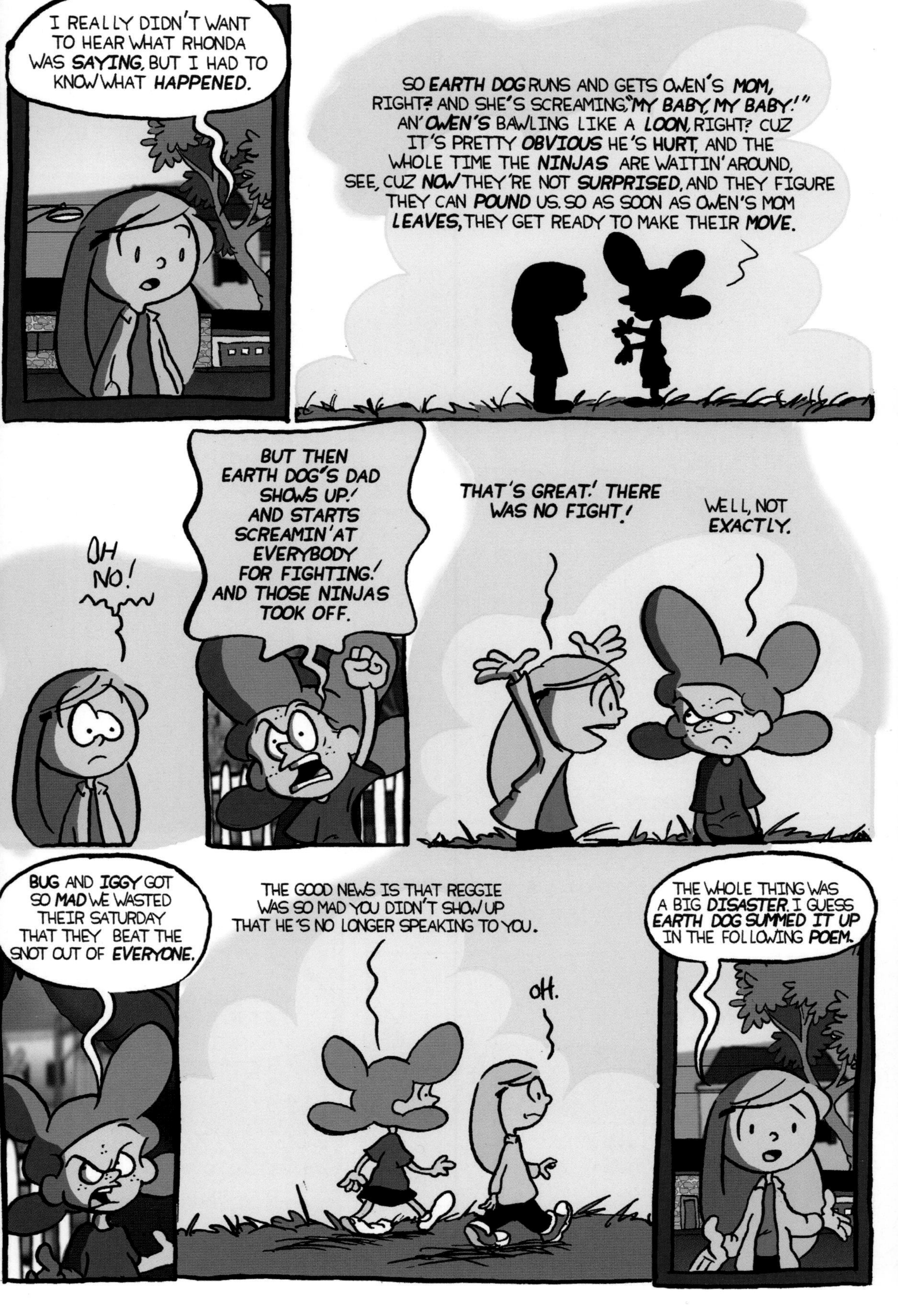
I REALLY DIDN'T WANT TO HEAR WHAT RHONDA WAS SAYING, BUT I HAD TO KNOW WHAT HAPPENED.
SO EARTH DOG RUNS AND GETS OWEN'S MOM, RIGHT? AND SHE'S SCREAMING, "MY BABY, MY BABY!" AN' OWEN'S BAWLING LIKE A LOON, RIGHT? CUZ IT'S PRETTY OBVIOUS HE'S HURT, AND THE WHOLE TIME THE NINJAS ARE WAITIN' AROUND, SEE, CUZ NOW THEY'RE NOT SURPRISED, AND THEY FIGURE THEY CAN POUND US. SO AS SOON AS OWEN'S MOM LEAVES, THEY GET READY TO MAKE THEIR MOVE.
OH NO!
BUT THEN EARTH DOG'S DAD SHOWS UP! AND STARTS SCREAMIN' AT EVERYBODY FOR FIGHTING! AND THOSE NINJAS TOOK OFF.
THAT'S GREAT! THERE WAS NO FIGHT!
WELL, NOT EXACTLY.
BUG AND IGGY GOT SO MAD WE WASTED THEIR SATURDAY THAT THEY BEAT THE SNOT OUT OF EVERYONE.
THE GOOD NEWS IS THAT REGGIE WAS SO MAD YOU DIDN'T SHOW UP THAT HE'S NO LONGER SPEAKING TO YOU.
OH.
THE WHOLE THING WAS A BIG DISASTER. I GUESS EARTH DOG SUMMED IT UP IN THE FOLLOWING POEM.

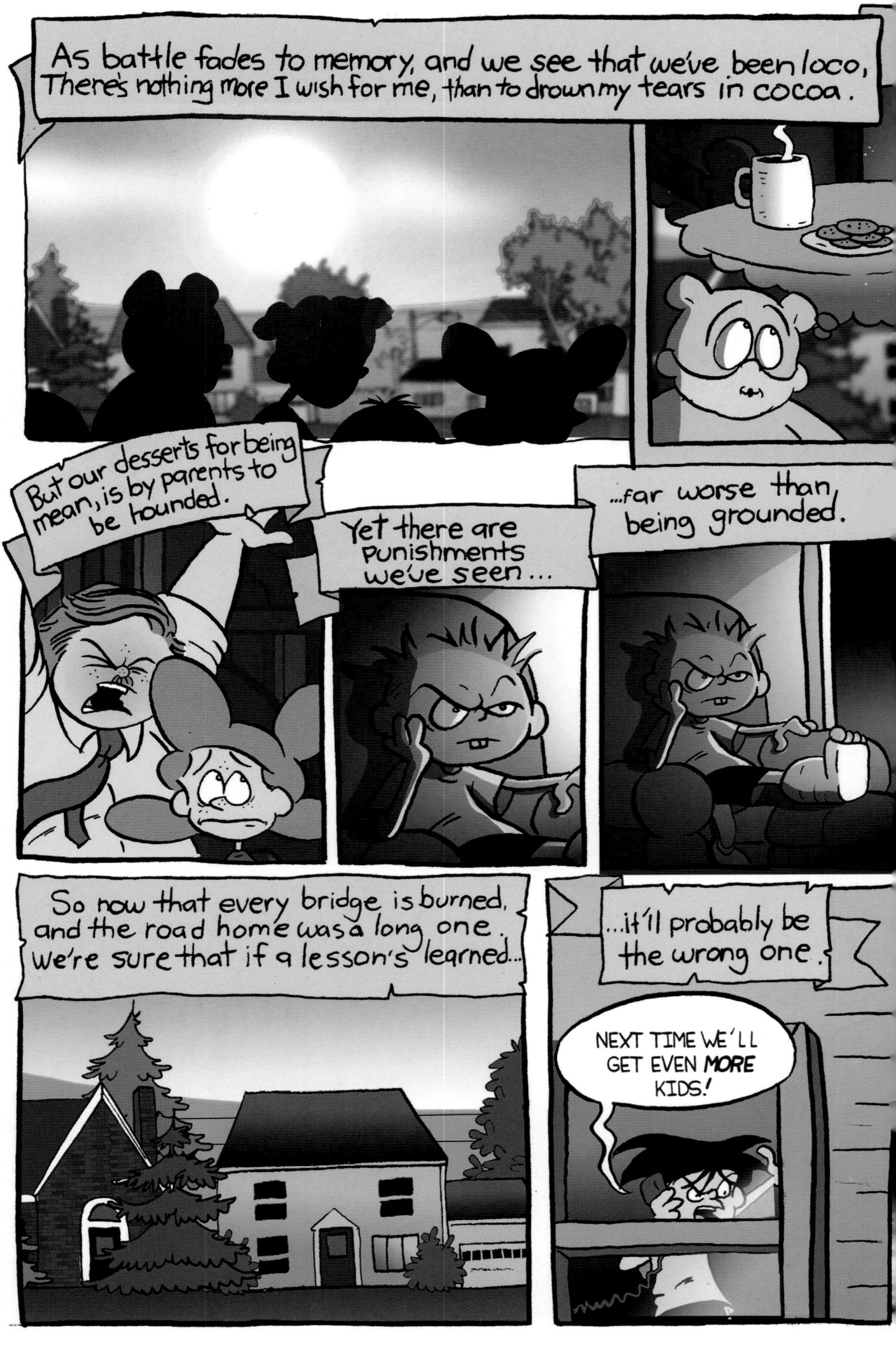
As battle fades to memory, and we see that we've been loco,
There's nothing more I wish for me, than to drown my tears in cocoa.
But our desserts for being mean, is by parents to be hounded.
Yet there are punishments we've seen...
...far worse than being grounded.
So now that every bridge is burned, and the road home was a long one.
We're sure that if a lesson's learned...
...it'll probably be the wrong one.
NEXT TIME WE'LL GET EVEN MORE KIDS!